CONTENTS

SUMMER FUN

TAQUANDRA JONESS

A JOURNALED JOURNEY

Summer Fun

Dedications

To My mother
This was written with love and in peace. With everything in me, you are forgiven. - Ladybug

To Bikel
This was written with all the strength you saw in me. I hope I have made you proud.

To Jerome

Thank You for the memories and love

To My Village
Thank you for playing your role and gluing together my broken pieces. Without your love and commitment my story surely would have ended differently.

To My Siblings
In the words of T.I. "We overcame the odds and did our thang".

To Poppa
It is like we always say, "Your Life, Your, Decisions".

To Dallas C. Gilbert
Thank you for the love, time, and patience. Thank you for unknowingly holding me together while I was internally in disarray. For the support given and the experienced distance. In all four seasons, we still.

To Camden T. Gilbert
We will not allow the world to tell our story, we have a voice of our own. When you want to know the story of your mother, read this in its entirety. Learn the lessons and apply them as you see fit. You are the embodiment of my reason and the Lords love Manifested. For you, I will.

On behalf of the children of the Crack Era

The children who were sacrificed for an unmeasurable high and the all mighty dollar

Sacrificed by the United States government, systemic racism and young hustlers looking for a come up

The King Pen, corner boys, street runners and lookouts

The dope dealers who single handedly decided their finances were more valuable than our mothers

The children who were subjected to mourn the loss of living relatives

The children who were required to survive in an environment in which they were not supposed to thrive

The drug was new, money moved fast, and our neighborhoods were traps

Our parents were victims

Victims of the system. Victims of their reality. Victims of undiagnosed mental health maladies.

With every rock they coped they voluntarily unconsciously solidified our inheritance of victimhood

All we ever did was arrive without consent
We recognize the power of the drug and realize you are sick

Seek Help
Get Well Soon.
-Children of the 80

Foreword

From My first memory of Naomi, I knew she was destined for greatness. She possesses the strength, tenacity, and character it takes to be successful in this world. The Various vicissitudes vocalized in this work, is a testament to her perseverance. Since childhood she has protected her family, carried the burdens of her parents, while acknowledging she was the product of their sin. Nevertheless, she has flourished where others failed, overcoming obstacles some could only imagine. This work captures the pain, suffering, and agony of this flower blooming through the concrete.

I cannot recall ever meeting Joness, as far as I can recall she was always there, however I truly met this queen when I was thirteen years old. We were attending AAU championship Track meet, and I was excited, anxious and all around scared out of my mind for what I believed to be the biggest moment of my childhood. You see, I finally was considered a "Big Boy" and I was representing the legendary Trailblazer track club. I was following in the footsteps of many team champions who had come before me and I had a responsibility to be competitive, make finals and at least come in one of the Top three places to qualify for the AAU Jr. Olympics.

The difference between my predecessors and me was I had no company. I was the only 13-year-old boy on the team, which means I had no relay teams or anything to fall back on. I had qualified to compete in the 100M hurdles, 200M hurdles, 400M and Triple Jump. I was nervous; the amount of pressure placed on us was like coal being pressed on by the earth to form a diamond. I felt small, unprepared and like a boy amongst men. That is when I met Joness. She came to me as if she could smell the fear that was residing inside of me. She calmly said, "Alright cousin, this is what we came to do; it's time to man up." Now this statement was a common figure of speech often spoken by her father, but she did not stop there. She continued, "We been preparing for this all year, let's go get it!"

We? We! We is what I needed to hear. It reminded me that while I was competing in individual events, this experience was shared with my entire community. I was not alone, I was not unprepared, and I was not small. I had trained for this moment, prayed for this moment, skipped social events for this moment. My family had invested their time and money into ensuring that I was successful. Joness specifically had given me countless pep talks, massages, and tough love to make sure I was prepared for this day. I was ready, and her words had reignited the fire within me to win. It was that day that I became a four-time medalist and qualified for the Jr. Olympics for the first time in my life. Since that day, her words have rung loudly in my mind anytime I encountered a battle.

Joness' ability to inspire, many times unbeknownst to her is a supernatural gift.

Although, we are only a few years apart in age I have always looked up to her. I watched her survive a stepmother, who at times seemed to despise her; a mother, who was not often there due to addiction; a school system that ways not created for her success and a life born with the odds stacked against her. I watched her, carry the weight of it all, day after day with poise and grace. Sometimes she carried it with tears in her eyes but every day she survived.

I understood the weight. Our lives paralleled in so many ways! My father also battled with addiction and after the passing of my sister, it seemed as if my family lost our king for good. The streets had him in an entanglement that he did not have the strength to defeat. To a child grieving the loss of a sibling this makes no sense. How can you not love your sons and daughters enough to stay clean? Do you realize what we are being left subject to? For me, that was Roy Hagens. The stepfather whose soul desire was to beat the sissy out of me. I was too soft, my lisp was un-appealing, my walk was not masculine enough, my conversation was not street enough, and my being was not good enough. For every beating, bruise, cursing and ridiculing there was darkness infused to a once bright light fighting to kill all hope in my life. He wanted to destroy me and by the time he was finished I was willing to do it for him. However, Joness would not let that be. Whenever Joness would come around, he would leave me alone to be the nice loving uncle. I was astonished every time, in utter disbelief that the same man that punched me in the head, rebuked my every word could show love. I longed for that power. One that could make even the coldest cruelest demons, show love and kind-ness, if even for a moment.

The strength that she exuded left me mesmerized. How could someone with the same crisis, trauma, and struggles as me appear so happy? How could she continue to love and inspire others? How was it that her situation did not destroy her, when every day I was sinking deeper into the darkness of night? Looking back on it, I believe subconsciously we applied the rules of track & field to every facet of our life. "Man – Up, we were prepared for this"

Before I was old enough to realize it, Joness had blazed a trail through the matrix of my life. Providing consistent examples of triumph amid adversity. Joness showed me that despite our situation, we are strong, courageous, expressive, and divinely black beings who can walk with our heads held high even when our world is in utter chaos.

This memoir is Joness' gift to all of us. Her life, her story, her triumphs, and her storms. Spoken in her authentic voice, loud, bold, jubilant, angry, and emotional like only she can. As you read this work, press beyond the surface, allow yourself to feel the ups, downs, twists, and turns that come with her story. Allow yourself to feel every emotion, triggered on the inside of you, knowing it was created in love, to inspire you.

-   Larenz Johnson

Naomi Nichelle Pratt

March 25, 1990

I think I am ready to talk

My life, from my perspective

Because some people are fortunate enough to meet their better half, grow in love and look forward to reproducing with one another. Unfortunately, this was not the case in my conception. These two people were not head over heels in love and this was not that rainbow and roses love story. I was born in March of 1990. Count nine months prior to, that makes our setting May/ June 1989. I. Me. My entire life and actual existence are the result of a little Summer Fun. No, my parents were not overtly enamored with one another. According to my grandmother, they were stoned, delusional and in denial.

Dear Sista Soulja, Thanks for the courage to
tell my story how it happened
-Joness

On July 20, 2019 I began my tenure at Blanche Ely High School as the Head Athletic Trainer. Along with this title I served as a permanent substitute teacher on the campus. This union allowed me to secure consistent supplemental income and become well acquainted with the campus, athletes, and general student body alike. As the athletic trainer I am responsible for providing medical coverage to each athlete for every sport within the school. In doing so I oversee prevention, treatment, rehabilitation, and emergency response at all sporting events. Within the first month on campus, I quickly became affectionately known as "Ma". My formal athletic training background primarily encompasses concentration on skeletal muscle, neuromuscular, and soft tissue injuries. However, in the past twelve months I have found myself acting more as a mother, counselor and mentor. These students, my newly founded unsolicited children were all in need of me. They all needed a fresh sounding board. Someone they felt comfortable enough to vent to. Someone who is young enough to understand their plights and old enough to help direct a clear path. They all bring their troubles and worries with them onto campus each day and often struggle navigating their real-world problems, emotions and required assignments. As a result, they come searching for me. No matter the time of day, my office serves as their hospital. There, they receive the love, time, attention and care they all are so desperately in need of. Throughout this first year I have had children snatched from their homes by the court system, children physically abused by their parents (and no not a whooping), young ladies experiencing their first heart breaks and others who were actually raped. In January of 2020 A young man from our rival high school sadly lost his battle with depression and committed suicide. He stepped in front of an oncoming train. The following Monday, five of my students reported to my office, their hospital, and stated that they often imagine doing the same. Ending it all. The pain. The drama. The constant unrealistic expectations for people in their circumstances. Coming from where they are from, their neighborhood, and such familial backgrounds they often cannot see their way out. In their lives There is a scarcity of persons who have attained a higher education, people rarely leave their neighborhood, and they often voice high school is a trap. As much as they have grown to love and respect me, they typically combat all advice I give with statements such as, "But Ma you're different". "you're not like us". "But you went to college and got your master's degree so you wouldn't understand". "But Ma, you straight, you had a nice family". Weekly, I am charged with reminding them that although I seem to have it all together, which I do not, I came from the same humble beginnings. I attended a Historically black high school in the heart of the inner city just like theirs. I experienced familial drama and trauma just like them and as a result at times found myself struggling academically. Their stories are relatable because I can personally relate. I am the product of a crack addicted mother and an alcoholic father. Based on who I come from and as a result what I have had to go through and grow through I am not supposed to be here. Based on the statistics, one would have counted me out for success long ago. I am currently a 30-year-old female African American athletic trainer. I have attended three universities, attained a master's degree and currently building my resume for my desired salary. On paper, I am not qualified enough to attain the position I have been preparing for. On paper, according to the numbers I am not supposed to make it to the next level. On paper, I am not qualified enough for the position I am currently in... But God. Doors have been opened before and I know they were not the last. So, I can stay here and fold to the facts or continue to step out on faith. I know the Lord is not through with me yet, I just pray I am prepared for the forthcoming blessings. I have said it before and I will say it again, thank God I don't look like my story but I'm sure happy I'm here to tell it. In this season in my life, I have the opportunity to help the forthcoming generation through their troubling seasons. Through my trials and tribulations, I have become equipped enough to understand that we must all develop effective coping mechanisms, create functional outlets and every now and then experience a healthy cry. As much as I have attempted to assist in helping them in this past year it was not practical for me to share my life's story with each student individually. Instead, I have decided to write. I am placing my life, my troubled past, darkest thoughts, and deepest fears on paper. With this I will also provide proof that there is greater on the other side. Through God, an established resilience and family either built or by blood we can all escape our current reality. So, to my children, the son I've birthed along with my adopted tribe, this is for you. My journey and how I made it over.

THE RECKONING

Picture it, Tampa, Summer of 1989 in the midst of the crack era. There is dope moving, money being made, and families being created and destroyed all in the same instant. Her name is Orjury Jordon, and she is "That Girl" as my daddy has always described her. The black cheerleader with the knocked knees, big smile, bigger booty and larger than life personality. She was a former student at ""THE"" Tuskegee Institute, and she got caught up in this thing called crack. I know she is not the only one. It is one or two or ten in every family. This one just happened to be my mother. At the age of 25 years old she just moved back home and had been enjoying time with a childhood acquaintance David Pratt, one of the neighborhood dope dealers and standout neighborhood athletes. It is June, it is hot, and you know how summer is, its sundress season. Two grown people got together and did what grown people do. Nine months later I was forced into this whirlwind hellhole we call earth and I have been fighting for greatness ever since. I just have one question for those two, "was it worth it?"

It was Sunday March 25, 1990 and the story is she went into false labor every Sunday prior to in that month. I know, just dramatic. A trait I inherited honestly. I finally decided to arrive and have not heard the end of it to this day. Apparently, she had complications during labor and supposedly "flat lined" and of course it was my fault. In her words, "I lost life giving it to you. 1. I did not ask to be here. 2. Do you remember dying? Anyway, I was surrounded by love. In attendance was my grandmother, grandfather, aunts, and godmothers. Unfortunately, like many other fathers David Pratt did not make an appearance. That is okay, the people who were there that day have been ever since. I was brought home to my grandmother's house and showered with love and affection. How do I know this you ask? I remember being a spoiled brat. I believe I am a lot better today although others may beg to differ. Although Orjury had already had her run in with the highly addictive substance, to my knowledge at this point in my life she had gotten clean. My earliest memories of her are exceptionally positive. I remember a strong woman, I remember love, I remember a mother.

David D. Pratt. Notice I have not mentioned him too often. I have always known him. I know who he is. I have his last name. We have had visitations sporadically throughout my life, but I never developed a relationship with him. As a child I remember being afraid of him. When he would enter the room, I would literally cry and experience shortness of breath. What all of that was about, I have no clue. Most likely that dramatic trait I picked up from my mother, but I digress. Throughout my childhood this man lived literally behind me. I could walk out of my back door and look into his backyard. And still I remember years where I saw him maybe twice. To date, he is older, more settled and attempting to get to know me. It is interesting, 30 years later and now we have time. I know I have had some spiritual growing to do to allow a relationship to develop but we are working on it.

So now that y'all know who they are, that is enough about them. This is my story.

When I was three years old my mother met Gerry Walton. He Was a widower and in the midst of raising two boys of his own. You know how that goes. Boy meets the girl. Boy marries girl. Girl gets pregnant and they live happily ever after, right? Wrong. Things were just about to start getting interesting. Even still, this meeting and relationship is the greatest gift she has ever given me. Through this union I found my family.

To my earliest recollection we began spending the night with my new family rather quickly. With my new Daddy Gerry and my two new brothers Gerry and Christian and the newest addition to our family, our baby sister Taylor, life was as it should be. We were living the "American Dream". We were being raised in a Two parent household in an upper middle-class neighborhood. Both of our parents were working professional jobs, we were being reared the "right way" and life was simple. In all the beauty, I still have early memories of familial distinction. My daddy had chosen my mother and me as his own. Even prior to Taylor's arrival we were all a unit. As young as I was, my memories span far. Daddy's parents, Grandma and Granddaddy Walton were not necessarily excited about this new relationship. I would often overhear conversations about bringing Gerry and Christian to visit them without me, and them questioning why I could not go and visit one of my other family members on nights they needed babysitters. Later in life I had a come to Jesus moment and realized this aided in me wanting to be wanted. I fashioned my actions accordingly and tried my best to be the model citizen at an early age. If it is a problem that I'm around just for the sake of my existence, I damn sure don't want to give them(anybody) any added reasons why I shouldn't be here. Mind you, these nights were not too often. They rarely let us out of their sight. We did EVERYTHING together. We traveled, experienced, and gained exposure to new adventures and ideals together. They took us to church, HBCU homecomings, talent shows, family vacations out of the county and Freaknik. Yes, FREAKNIK! We were markedly the youngest group of persons in attendance, but we were in attendance. There, and Black Beach Week. together, they decided that they were not going to stop living their lives just because they had children. So, they brought us along for the ride. We would spend one day with our mother and the ladies. The next we would spend with daddy and the guys. Both nights, they would order us a pizza and leave us in the hotel room and dare us to leave under any circumstances. Back then, in pretherapy, no rationalization, or conversations with children type of world, the last thing we ever wanted to do was be the example. Our parents believed in corporal punishment and Orjury even more than our daddy. Daddy would spend most of his time trying to save us from being in trouble with mama. Nevertheless, we all made it. We all survived and became productive citizens in society. The whoopings we received were 98% of the time well deserved and although she has done some shit in her life, I can and will give credit where credit is due. We knew early just where the line of misbehavior was drawn and not to cross it. That line has followed us until this day. That line demanded respect of self and others, required us to hold elders at a high regard and served as a constant reminder that there are always consequences to our actions. In 1995 they tied the knot. It was a beautiful day. One that I will never forget. She planned the entire thing with her family. She envisioned a "Coming to America" theme and made it happen. Our grandmother along with a few of her closest friends made each of the bridesmaid dresses and every cummerbund and tie. The morning of the wedding I remember waking with my mother in the hard rock hotel on Hillsborough avenue. With a full morning ahead of us we took off towards the salon prepping hair and nails and perfecting the look. Afterwards we rushed towards the church. The ceremony was to be held at New Mount Zion M.B. Church, my daddy's family church. In the dressing room all the women corralled ensuring that Orjury was dressed to perfection. They ensured her makeup was tasteful and every hair was properly in place. In all this commotion I remember feeling uncomfortable and overwhelmed. Up until that point I had never been surrounded by those women, my women, (my family and godmothers) and all the attention was directed somewhere other than myself. Like how dare she attempt to be prettier than I was. I was crushed. I spent two hours before the wedding crying. Like real tears. I was hurt. Not at the fact that she was getting married. That was cool with me. I loved my daddy, and I loved my brothers. I just could not believe that she had the audacity to be more important than me in those moments. Like why are you all paying her so much attention? I'M right here. Hello! Could you believe she had the gall, the nerve, the gumption to walk out of that dressing area in this big, beautiful gold and white gown. I had on a cute little dress; it was nice. (Mind you she had it made specifically to match hers). But it wasn't hers. It did not demand the attention that hers did. I felt so betrayed. You have all these people coming here, to watch and witness and you are taking all the attention for yourself. True it was her wedding day, but the attention should have been mine. She calmed me down just long enough to assure me that I was just as pretty as she was. Her patience was impeccable that day. On a regular day, Normal Orjury, regular every day in her right mind Orjury would have whooped me and went on about her day. On this day she tried her hardest to keep cool. And she did, until she did not. That is when I knew it was time to stop the crying. That is what was in my best interest.

That evening I walked down the aisle hand in hand with both of my brothers, as I have in every endeavor of my life since that day. We were preceded by an array of bridesmaids and groomsmen. The sanctuary was packed. People came from all over to bear witness to my parents declaring their love for each other and our family in front of God and man. They exchanged vows, exchanged rings and both placed rings on our fingers to signify the unifying of our blended family. Later that night, the six of us rode in a stretch Lincoln town car to the IBEW building where my parents entered to Pattie LaBelle's Right Kinda Lover and we all danced the night away. This is to date, one of my fondest memories.

By this time, we had moved from my daddy's house in river grove to a four-bedroom, two-bathroom home in temple terrace. The boys had their own rooms, Taylor and I shared a room. Yet, I can count on one hand how many times I can remember us all sleeping apart. Every night we all convened in my room to sleep together. I had a big white Queen-sized bed with four huge columns. The bed depicted how my extended family and my parents had treated me my entire life. There was no reason a four-year-old little girl needed such lavish sleeping arrangements. However, they made sure I understood that I am queen, and always will be. I was accustomed to being treated well, shown affection, and knowing that I am loved. Anything less, is unacceptable. Anyway, I never complained about the extra space in my bed. It only guaranteed there was plenty of space for all my siblings. If there was a night, we slept apart it was only because we were in trouble and that was our punishment or one of the adults was having a bad day and being petty by taking their frustrations out on us innocent children.

I do have a few memories of my overt bratty behavior getting the best of me. In our earliest moments I did not enjoy the outside, thought it a crime to be subjected to walking through grass and if any activity required me to break a sweat it was not on the top of my to do list. Once I began joining my new family out at Grandma Jackson's house (a staple in our familial history) these habits I had to soon break. All the 15 or so kids would be outside jumping, running, kicking, and climbing. I rather enjoyed this time. It was awesome seeing them enjoying themselves as I watched out of the front window. I just knew they (the adults) did not want me to go out and engage in such activities. But to no avail, there was Auntie Ari. She refused to allow me to stand in the window and just watch. One day she drug me out of the house and forced me to join in a game of kickball with the others and the rest was history. Grandma Jackson's house was in Thonotosassa. The country. At her house we were only allowed to drink milk and water, after school snacks were to be consumed in the kitchen and we were locked outside for at least three hours a day. Her cats ate better than us, she ignored us like a pro, and I am sure we got on her everlasting nerve. Picture it, 15-20 children aged 11 and under all being watched by one 75-year-old woman. As an adult now that I think about it, I think it was geriatric abuse, but it was the best time of our lives. During this time, we climbed trees, scrapped our knees, and got in trouble collectively. At this point in my life, I had the pleasure of spending time with one of my best friends. Our cousin Brielle. She was Auntie Ari's only girl and the oldest female grandchild. She was everything to me. She was beautiful, athletic, girly but a tomboy. Sweet but had plenty of sass and youthful with an old soul. Daily she drug me out of my naturally reserved shell. She forced me into the field to play, required me to conduct myself with confidence and insisted that there was nothing the boys did that we were not able to do and better. According to her, we could play football, wrestle and pee standing up just like them. During our customary time of being locked outside, when nature called, we would typically squat by a tree to relieve ourselves. This way we would be able to continue to play without being locked inside. One day, she got the bright idea that if the boys can catch a tree without having to squat so could we and she was determined for us to be able to do the same. Imagine two adolescent girls attempting to pee on a tree and practicing aiming like the boys. There was urine all over our pants and legs. As awful as it was, these were the good old days. We ran down dirt roads, jumped on the neighbor's trampoline and raced in the street. You know, all things pre-technology. Between the 5-6 sets of children, we all fought, laughed, cried, placed blame, and complained like the best of them. Grandma Jackson was our mutual enemy and we all loved her just the same. One day, Grandma Jackson piled us up into her car, interrupting our playing, and drove us to Winn dixie. Once we got there, she made us sit in the car. We were all furious. How dare she make us ride with her to the grocery store and make us wait in the car. We could have been at the house enjoying ourselves still. Irritated, Brielle had the great idea to put boogers on the back of her headrest while she was in the store. It was genius. Picture it, a group of children sitting in a car digging up their noses and wiping their fingers on the back of a headrest. Brielle even dug up her baby brother's nose to get his contribution. She was my hero. Once grandma Jackson returned, we were elated. We laughed all the way back to the house and then got in trouble because she could not figure out what was so funny. At grandma Jackson's house we all fell in love with the new Whitney Houston movie "The Bodyguard". We all memorized each song and would practically put on a show every afternoon. Once daddy caught wind of these actions, he had a brilliant idea to form our own rap/dance group so we could "blow up" and be bigger than the Jackson 5. His logic was, if we could remember the words to the songs in the movie, we should also be able to remember whatever songs he created for us. And that is exactly what we did. Daddy went into the lab creating beats and stringing together lyrics to aid in personifying our larger-than-life stage personalities. He finalized the first single and just like that we were now a rap/dance group. My brothers and I were now the members of CNM. Master C (Christian), Lady Ni' (Naomi) and G-Money (Gerry). Shake Your Money Maker was our first single. We performed in local talent shows, at the boys and girls club and on large stages. We had wardrobes, rehearsals, and a promotion team. Our family was pushing our cassettes out of the back of their trunks like it was the highly addictive substance crack. We took pictures, signed autographs, and made appearances. We were slowly becoming local celebrities. We opened for the Kings of Comedy, Mystical, The Puppies and did a signing with Immature. We were the "IT" children. We were the first ones with J's, performed at nightclubs and conducted interviews on the radio. They were priming us for a life of stardom. In 1995, we auditioned to perform on ShowTime at the Apollo. We won the local competition and in March of 1996 appeared on Apollo Kids.

During this time, we attended Thonotosassa elementary school. My first day was the beginning of kindergarten. Ms. Parker's class. I walked onto campus with my brothers and cousins. That day was my first at the school and I was in trouble within the first hour. First and only time, but hey, there is a first time for everything. We walked into the lunchroom for breakfast. One of the only times in history we were on campus early enough for breakfast. As we were standing in line a brown skinned girl approached us with the biggest smile and happiest greeting. My big brother explained to me that she was his girlfriend. Without hesitation, a second thought or look, I kicked her. How dare she think she is MY brother's girlfriend. Why does he need her? Why would he want her? Mind you, they had to have been in no more than the fourth grade and their relationship meant nothing more than friends, even still I was furious. To my surprise the principal was in the lunchroom at that time and witnessed the entire moment. She grabbed my hand and marched me to Ms. Parker's class. No breakfast, no conversation. At that moment I knew I had written a ticket Orjury would not be afraid to cash, but it was okay with my life. Just know, after that interaction and the forthcoming repercussions, I never had a disciplinary issue on that campus again. I did however receive my last individual whooping because of a spelling test at that school a few years later. By that time, I was in the second grade and in Ms. Acosta's class. Our class was assigned ten spelling words every Monday and charged with completing a spelling test the following Friday afternoon. Each night of the week, as a family we would gather around our grand dining room table, complete homework, and receive feedback from our parents as they reviewed our work. We practiced spelling words by saying the word, spelling the word, and repeating the word again. After completing this routine for four days, come Friday, I would ace the test each week. One week, our routine suddenly changed. We were not reminded to sit to the table and complete our work and neither parent practiced with us nor asked to review our words. So, I didn't. That week I went into that spelling test completely unprepared, and it showed. For the first time that year, I received an unsatisfactory score on my spelling test. Of the ten words provided, only two were correct. I walked into the lunchroom that day a big ball of tears. Chloe, our adopted cousin, walked up to me and asked me what was wrong. I replied, "I failed my spelling test, and my mama is going to whoop me". I knew what time it was. Just earlier that year I witnessed her whoop my big brother for Christmas treeing a practice test. Her exact words, "I do not care if it is a practice test, real test or pop quiz. You apply yourself 100% every single time". So, this failed real spelling test was about to get my ass beat. Chloe tried to calm me down and patted my back all the way through the lunch line. That afternoon, like every other paper I received that year, I crumbled up that test and threw it into the bottom of my bookbag. I got home that evening and my mother asked me, "How did you do on your spelling test"? Before I knew it, a lie flew out of my mouth as easy as it was for me to breath. "I got 100". She congratulated me and gave me a big hug. She did not need proof because it was not hard to believe. I Did receive 100%, every other week. That next morning, on a random Saturday, she woke me up and said we were going out on a girl's day. Excited, we got dressed and prepared ourselves for a day of shopping. A few hours later Auntie Ari and her crew showed up to the house and we went our separate ways. Daddy took himself and the boys up to The University of South Florida for a few games of basketball while mama and Auntie Ari took Chloe and I out on the town. That day we shopped until we could not shop anymore. We stopped by Red Lobster for lunch and returned to the house to make more room in the trunk for a round two of shopping. During our shopping intermission we had all reconvened at the house. The boys were in the living room crowded around our big screen tv playing Sega genesis. We ran in to drop our bags and decompress for a few moments before we ran back out into the streets. Out of nowhere, and in front of everybody, Chloe yelled, "Naomi, did you get your whooping yet"? I was pissed. The fuck was she thinking? Like, girl you been with me all day. You could have asked me that when it was just the two of us. If I would have gotten my whooping, do you really think we would have been out on this shopping spree all damn day? I was so over her. My mama and daddy both looked at me with the quickness. Mama said, "What whopping"? I replied, "I have no clue what she is talking about". Chloe with her insistent self said, "yes you do. Remember you were crying in the lunchroom yesterday because you failed your spelling test, and you said your mama was going to whoop you". I rolled my eyes harder than I had ever rolled them before. So, you want me to die? Like, you must be ready to be mourning my death, at my funeral, this time next week. She knew that lady was going to kill me, and she made sure she heard it. My mama called me into the kitchen calmly. "Naomi, if you tell me the truth now, I will not be mad. Just tell me the truth and we can go on with our day". I could not believe she would look me dead in my eyes and lie to me like that. I wasn't sure what kind of dummy she took me for, but I wasn't falling for it. So, I met her right where she was. Since we in here lying to each other I'll keep up my end of the lie. "No ma'am, I don't know what she's talking about. I got an A on my test just like I do every week". She said okay and seemed to let it go. We left the house again and continued our day of shopping. Later that evening after we were exhausted and unwinding, we were in her room and she suggested we begin to take my hair out. I sat on the floor happy and continent as my mother began to unravel my poetic justice plaits and comb through my thick mane. A few moments later she said, "Lady, go get your bookbag so we can clean it out while we are doing this". I hopped up and skipped my naive ass across the hall to grab my bookbag out of my room. I sat back down between her legs and began to pull each paper out. She said with an overly sweet voice, "and unfold all of the balled-up papers and place them on the bed next to me". I complied and after about three pieces of balled up paper it suddenly dawned upon me, that damn test is in here. I slowed down to a turtle's pace. I was sitting there trying to figure out how I would pull off bypassing that specific piece of paper. A few moments later, it was too late. She saw the test and dropped the comb immediately. "Get the belt and go to your room". I was terrified. She went ballistic. "How dare you lie to me"! According to her, I was receiving a whopping for the lie I told and not the grade itself. The audacity of her to want to whoop me for doing the exact same thing she had done. She lied to me earlier that day in the kitchen and she was lying to me then. If I had come home and told her my grade, she would have whooped me immediately. All I did was push it back about thirty-six hours. She was enraged and displaying an anger I had never witnessed. Crying hysterically on the bed I belted out, "I'm getting scared of you like David Pratt". She hit me so hard with that belt. I had received whoopings before and I knew to just lay there and take it. This time, for some foolish reason, I grabbed the belt. I grabbed it and held on with everything in me. She slung me all around that room. She threw me into one of the posts on my bed and cracked it at its base. She drug me across the carpet until I had a carpet burn. I screamed, "I gotta pee"! As I did during every whooping. Whenever I got nervous that was the immediate feeling. Typically, they would let me up to pee sooner than later and that would be the end of it. This time, she stepped back, and told me to go pee. I sat on that toilet contemplating my life decisions for what seemed like an eternity. She yelled, "Hurry up"! I was so confused, what could she possibly want with me now? I got up slowly and returned to my room. She stepped from behind my door and swung the belt again. I was in disbelief. This bitch really took an intermission on a whopping. I am not sure how long we were in that room but what I do know is when we walked in there, daddy was not home. During the whooping he had returned home, and he says he had been there for ten minutes and I was still getting beat. He walked in trying to get her off me. "Alright Orjury, that's enough. It's over". They began to wrestle over the belt, and he got her out of my room. She walked out calmly and went into her bedroom. As daddy turned to go up front, she sprinted back across the hall into my room with the belt, locked my door and proceeded to continue whooping me. I was devastated. During her "whooping speech", y'all know what I am talking about, she explained that she was upset that I had compared her to David Pratt. Again, as a child I was terrified of him. At that moment, she was giving me every reason to be terrified of her. Then whopped me for trying to explain my emotional intelligence. My cousin RoShard had to use a butter knife to pry the lock open so they, my daddy and cousin, could wrestle her off me once again. They got her out, locked my door and closed it behind them. I had to be locked away from my mother for my own safety. Laying on the bed crying I heard her grab her keys and slam the front door. She disappeared for most of that night. That night, I dreamed about that whooping, got nervous in my sleep, and peed in the bed. The next morning, I got whooped for wetting the bed and THAT was my last whooping. After that, anything that even sounded like it wasn't in line with what we were supposed to be doing I wanted no parts of.

It was around this time that we were all forced into a familial bond so tight that till this day, people still cannot understand. Daddy always led our family like a coach and ensured that we were a team. If we all play our positions correctly and unselfishly, we will always prosper. Unfortunately, my mother could not sustain her role. Somewhere along this fairytale she lost her footing and began using crack again. Up until this point she was to our knowledge, clean and living accordingly. She had a great position at Tampa Electric Company and was active in our family, community, and a great partner in her relationship. One day it all changed, and the roles shifted. She began disappearing, acting funny and there was this constant stench in our house coming from her room. I noticed it only occurred when daddy was not around. Daddy and I have always had a special bond. We Have always talked about everything. So, it was imperative that I asked him what was going on. Not sure how it happened or the exact date, but he eventually broke the news to us that our mother was addicted to crack. He believed in being upfront with us. My grandmother, Orjury's mother, was angry that he would share such information with us. She believed in keeping children in children's places. By no means did we think we were grown but according to daddy, if we were to survive the demon living amongst us, we would all have to be knowledgeable about what was going on so we could hold everyone accountable and assist in her rehab. For means of survival, at the age of five, I was forced to take on the mothering role ensuring my siblings and daddy were always okay. At the age of nine Gerry was daddy's best friend. He was old enough to understand fully what was going on and was there to guide us when need be. Christian was four and always our comedic relief. He has somehow always known how to keep us happy and smiling even in our darkest days. Taylor was still a baby. So, there we were. Daddy and his four horsemen as he has deemed us.

Living the American dream in a silent hell. Our lives were being torn apart at the seams by my mother and no matter what tactics the adults employed, she was determined to tear it all apart. We were still traveling, performing, and trying to conduct business as usual. However, these things begin to suffer when the backbone breaks. She lost her job, began to miss dinners, stopped reviewing homework, and would randomly disappear. Our things began to disappear slowly but surely. She took our rings they gave us at their wedding one day and stated she was going to clean them. We never saw our rings again. Heading home from school one day we rode past a group of men standing on the corner. I noticed a man had on a Chicago bulls' jacket just like my brother's. We got home and checked his closet and to no avail it was missing. She had given it to one of the dope boys as payment for her most recent high. Daddy had to place her on an allowance trying to save her from herself. If you do not have any finances to fund your habit it should suffer right? She taught us. In our driveway at one point, we had a Lincoln town car, BMW, Mercedes Benz, jeep, and her Toyota corolla. We would leave her home during the day as we are off in school and at work. This would obviously require one vehicle. We would return in the evening to an empty driveway. Due to her lack of funds, she began renting our vehicles out to the neighborhood dope dealers in exchange for her fix. It was so bad I began to wish that she would just disappear. Do you know how awful a situation must be for a young girl to wish that her mother would leave and never return? The woman who carried me. Nurtured me and had gotten me to that point. I was over her. At the young of 5 I had to realize who was for me and who was against me. She was obviously against me. She was against us. She was taking from everything we were trying to build. All that we were attempting to be. She valued herself and her raggedy ass high over all of us. She was selfish. She was untrustworthy. She was no longer the woman I loved and respected. Do not get me wrong. I love the lady. Today, right now. There is a love that will never be broken, but it has never been the same. I remember seeing Mel's hotdog sign on Busch Blvd. every night heading home. It took us approximately 3 minutes to reach our home from there. I would close my eyes tight and pray as hard as I could silently, "Please don't be home. Please don't be home". If she would just leave, we could all be happy again. But of course, that would be too much like right. Daddy tried all he could to help her straighten up. He paid for rehab out of pocket. She left voluntarily. Took us with her to NA meetings on Wednesday nights so she would feel supported in her journey. She stopped showing up. Like lady, what more do you want? What exactly are you looking for? Rock bottom?

One night we arrived home, as we were walking into the front door with daddy, she was walking out of their bedroom with a strange man carrying their television. Daddy blocked the front door and asked what was going on. She cried and begged my daddy to just let him take the television. She proclaimed that she owed him some money and he was there receiving his payment. Still, Daddy refused to let him leave with the television. The man placed it down and left the house. She cried and exclaimed that my father was wrong for not letting her settle her debt with this sketchy man. How dare she. All he was doing to keep us afloat as she slowly sank this ship, and you are upset that we will not happily agree with you giving our belongings away one by one for your own personal gain. The next night, in the car with daddy heading home we stopped at the 7-11 on Yukon and 40th St. Daddy left us in the car and ran into the store. As he was in the store a black car pulled up next to us. As usual, both of my brothers and sister were asleep. Not me. No matter the time, place, or occasion I ensured I was awake and daddy's riding partner. His sounding boards. The person he could vent to because we were the only ones who really knew the hell we were living through. As he came out of the store, I watched every step. A man hopped out of the black car parked next to us as my daddy approached his front door and placed a gun into his abdomen. It was the same man my daddy put out of our house the night prior to. I was stuck in disbelief. Trying my hardest to get my brother's attention I could not get my mouth to form the proper words. The only thing I could muster up was "Daddy". He made it into the car safely and unharmed, physically at least.

He was shaken. He had just had a gun drawn on him, in front of his children behind this woman and her ridiculous addiction. My daddy was not in the streets. He was a law-abiding man just attempting to do right by his family. He is not a saint in the least. However, he did not conduct himself in a manner that this would ever be our reality. On our way to the house, he explained to us that the man threatened to return to our home and "shoot it up". Once we arrived home, he instructed us to grab a few things from our rooms and come to his room immediately. My room, along with Christian's, was in the front of the house. Our parents' room was on the back side of the home. So here we were. Daddy and his four horsemen laying on the floor on the opposite side of his bed. He was attempting to protect us from the foolishness we were in. of course, on this night, my mother was nowhere to be found. For the next 30 nights we all slept there. On the floor. Together. We held onto each other for dear life. Praying that we would all make it until the next morning. Things began to slowly migrate towards normal for what normal was in our household. We eventually made it back to our regular sleeping arrangements and the fear of dying in our sleep was no longer in the forefront of our minds. Of course, things still went missing. Mama even broke a window out of our garage once, then called the police and reported that our Sega Saturn had been stolen. Like really lady? People broke in our home and out of all the things in here the game system was the only thing the robbers decided to take? On this day I realized how great of an actress my mother is. Talking to the police she was extremely convincing. I am talking speaking with conviction, worry, an ugly cry and in despair. If you did not know her you would never know she had pawned our gaming system for a piece of crack rock. The lady was good. On another occasion daddy had been working on the sound system in his Mercedes Benz. To know him is to know that out of all his vehicles, the Benz was his baby. It was his project. He had it painted green, and it flipped to look black at night. All white leather interior and hammer tires. The sound system was impeccable. You could hear us coming from a mile away. Outside of us, his kids, his Mercedes Benz was daddy's prize possession. Apparently, something was wrong with the system and he was waiting on a part to fix it. As he waited, he decided to drive the Lincoln in the meantime. This day, while we were all out of the house, she gave daddy's Benz to the dope boys. It was not the first time, but it was damn sure the last. What she and these egregious men were not aware of is that daddy had previously disconnected wires in the trunk. He did not bother putting them back together because he had no intention of driving it again until it was back in order. So, these men took off, in my daddy's car, stunting, I'm sure. A vehicle they could only afford to drive 2-3 hours at a time at the sake of our family and the future of an addicted woman. They pulled up to a corner store and hopped out like they were the boss my daddy actually was. One of the wires sparked against the metal in the trunk and the entire car went up in flames. His car, his baby was now burnt to a crisp. That afternoon we were picked up from school by our aunt. We pulled into our driveway to see this crispy car backed into its regular spot. We entered the house and my mother conducted herself like there was nothing wrong. Like she was not the root cause of this loss. Like she did not care that she had snatched something so meaningful from the man she claimed to love. That evening, my daddy did not come home. We were stuck there wondering, where he was, what he was doing and if he was still sane. He returned home the following afternoon. Later in life he explained to me that he drove to Orlando for the night because if he had come home that same day, he would have killed her. Our life went on like this for a few years. Daddy eventually placed a deadbolt lock on Christian's room and anything of importance that we cared to have once we returned home every day was placed in there. It was not too long after this incident that daddy decided that he had had enough. He could not take it anymore. For his sanity and safety, he had to leave her alone. Prior to leaving he asked her to bow out. He asked her to just leave us in the home so we could live peacefully without her added drama. He offered to raise all of us without child support or contention. She refused. She said if she could not live in our home, none of us would. Immature, selfish, and unethical. So, he left. I will never forget the day. He packed his things and my brothers and walked out of the front door. I had never cried so hard in my life. I held onto him so tightly begging him to take us with him. Unfortunately, if you remember, I am not his child biologically. Therefore, without her, I'm not his child legally. He could not just take me, and she refused to give him permission. Because he was forced to leave me, he left Taylor with me so I would not be alone. I have always thanked God that he did because I do not know if I would have survived her and all her forthcoming antics without my sister. So here we were. Me, Taylor, and the lady formerly known as our mother. I did not know who she was now. The lady they all left us with. The woman we favored. The woman who ran away 50 percent of my family. But my mother, she was not. She was not the woman I had grown to love, adore and admire. My daddy had always described her as one of the strongest women he knew. If that were the case, why couldn't she beat this habit? Why couldn't she choose us over that thing she seemed to love so much? Why had she allowed her own selfish needs to outweigh our wellbeing? So, we were there with her, whenever she was home. She began leaving us alone a lot often. The lights were off, there was no food in the fridge, and she began selling everything in our house at a much more rapid pace piece by piece. She was angry. She was mean and she seemed to despise our presence. That was cool with me. I was over her ass too. The feeling was definitely mutual. We saw our brothers each day in school. We weren't in the same grade, so it wasn't for extended periods of time, but we did see them. One morning in their first month of their separation I was called out of class to the guidance office. A strange white lady introduced herself and began asking me questions about our homelife. Where did I live? Who did I live with? Were we eating? Was there any illegal activity taking place in our home? Of course, coming from an African American home it is instilled in us at an early age "what happens in this house, stays in this house". So of course, I answered with the most politically correct answers possible. Yes ma'am. We are good. Lights are on. We are eating. We have the same familial dynamic I have always been accustomed to. You know, toxic shit. Sitting in that office lying my ass off protecting the woman who had obviously forfeited protecting me. At 9 years old I had already been programmed to internalize my true feelings for the sake of others. I had to forfeit my truth for what I felt the world needed to hear. In that hour-long meeting as a fourth grader, I had to make a rash decision for my sister and me. If I tell the truth, it would be beautiful if you just take us to my daddy. But y'all might try to put us in a foster home somewhere. Naw. y'all might try to separate us and claim it is what is best for us. I am straight. I had already become accustomed to the hell I had to endure every day. I was Not excited about trading my hell for another. As bad as home is, I still see my brothers. As much of a front as I must put on everyday coming to this school, I knew we would see daddy on the weekend. Ain't no telling what yall might have planned if I sit here and bare my soul. I am straight. I returned to class feeling like I had made the right decision. Once again being placed in that mothering position. Even if I'm not overjoyed, I'm still here for Taylor. Hell, she was still there for me. Although she was only in kindergarten at the time, she has been saving me long before she knew. That afternoon we were picked up by daddy. He asked if I had a visitor and what types of questions, she had for me. Apparently, she was sent to the school from the family court system because he was attempting to gain custody of us. Like, really? You tell me this now? If I would have known, it was you who sent her I would have told everything. I would have told her how when I wake up in the middle of the night she is nowhere to be found. I would have told her how she locks herself up in her room and that stank ass smell barrels from under her door all day. Or how I just do not feel safe with her. But no, I found out after the fact and I have already fucked up the plan. They proceeded with their divorce and no matter how much he explained to the court that she was not fit to sustain custody the raggedy ass court system and everyone involved insisted that the best place for young girls to be is in the care of their mother. Bitch. You come live with her then. This was not us being in the care of our mother. This was us being sacrificed for what they felt comfortable with. I am sure the show she put on in the courtroom did not help the argument against her either. I was not in attendance; however, I could only imagine the dramatics and stunts she put on for the Judge. At that moment in time, she still presented well-kept and put together. At first glance you would never know she was a rock a day kind of girl. I get it. Historically speaking the mother is typically the caregiver. The nurturer. The parental figure who provides necessary guidance with love and attentiveness. What they failed to do was show empathy. They did not place themselves in our shoes in an effort to make a reasonable and rational decision. No. They opted to foolishly rule in the mother's favor. There was no personable consideration, and it was generic. Cookie cutter. Cut and dry. They, the court system, left us in the custody of a crack addicted woman who was spiraling out of control and never gave a second thought about our wellbeing. In the words of my FAMU brother Skoota, "they were trying to break us". This world, these people. They did not want us to survive. They wanted us to break and burn and disappear into vapor just like the crack rock our mother voluntarily inhaled into her lungs. Little did they know we are comprised of all our mother's greatest attributes, our father's love, our grandparent's prayers, and resilience built only through turmoil. We are going to be stronger than the generational curses which were supposed to destroy us. We are going to do it differently this time around.

Fourth grade was a very eventful year. Not that any other year lacked in its dramatics, but fourth grade was the year of changes. During this year, my parents' divorce was finalized, school became my safe haven and the place I began to struggle, we were in our darkest place with our mother and nanny finally came to rescue us from what was once our beloved home. Eventually, nanny (Orjury's mother) did come and rescue us from the dark, dingy, damn near abandoned temple terrace home. We packed our clothes in four big black garbage bags and that was all she wrote. The house we knew as our home was no longer ours. There, we grew accustomed to four large bedrooms, two bathrooms, a large front yard, an in-ground swimming pool and neighbors who we knew as friends and eventually considered family. As we packed up and drove away it was freeing and capitulating all in the same instant. I thank God we were rescued, however, it felt like we had lost a long-fought war. Like all the effort and labor, we had put into keeping ourselves functioning and together for the past three years had been all for naught. As we pulled up on the corner of 37th and Hanna this was our new reality. Nanny's house is where I began my tenure here on this earth so in ten short years of life, I had just come full circle. This time, it was me, Taylor, and our mother all sharing one bedroom smaller than the one Taylor and I had previously shared. That was fine. We were with nanny. I felt safe. Lights were on, I slowly began to feel love again and there was not a scarcity of food. Although I had to get used to the fact that nanny did not mind bashing my daddy openly in front of us, everything else was markedly better. She would often call my daddy a weak man. On the phone, in front of us. Do you know what that does to the psyche of a nine-year-old girl who thinks the world of her father. Mentally and psychologically, I was stuck between a rock and a hard place. This place, nanny's house was now my refuge. She was our savior and cared enough to extend herself to assist in raising us. She was not obligated to do so and for this I was extremely grateful. I found myself feeling and living a life of AT LEAST. One of overt gratitude. Like I did not have to be here, so I must accept whatever I get with nothing less than a smile. Like AT LEAST you have a grandmother who was there. AT LEAST. But she insisted on bashing my daddy. And as much as it hurt, I could not express just how wrong it was without coming out of pocket or being considered a disrespectful child. She was convinced that he was a weak man because he divorced her child and left her in the pit she was determined to dig. I get it. That overprotective gene activated during childbirth is real. Like no matter what your children do or say or how wrong in life they are you are obligated to be on their side. But she had no clue what my daddy put up with trying to help save her child from herself. She was not there with us as we cried and prayed and attempted to protect her child. She

34

was not there when he begged her to fight for her family. She was not there when all we had was my daddy. When he did our hair in the mornings, got us dressed for school, as he ensured we felt whole amid being torn apart. I'm not discounting any interactions she has had to endure with her daughter throughout the years, but she called my daddy weak. Weak for leaving. Weak for hurting. Weak for not being afraid to cry. It was not until years later that she refrained from speaking such degrading statements about my daddy. By then, I was entering my preteen years and the attitude I harvested from all those moments would slowly come to a head later in life.

That year we attended Cahoon Elementary School. Ms. Troy was my teacher and to this day she has been my favorite. She was a younger African American lady who just seemed to get me. She could tell when I was struggling and although we never actually talked about what was going on at home, I felt she just knew the extra love and attention I needed that year. I was her classroom helper and would do anything she asked. She was strong and stern but understanding. She knew how to have fun but required her class to perform and operate at the highest of standards. She honestly reminded me of my mother B.C. (before crack). I began staying after school with her every day. Her class was my new haven. After school we would have a late lunch, clean the classroom, watch the stories, and listen to music. It was the most normal time of the day for me, and I valued it immensely. I hated to leave school each day. At times I wished I could just go home with her. In the middle of the school year my grades began to suffer. For the first time in history my grades were below average. Not in every subject, but for the first time I began to view math as my nemesis. It did not come to me as naturally as the commonsense of language arts, reading and social studies. With math, it required time, energy, and effort. Years prior to, we would all sit around at our grand dining room table to complete, study, and review our homework with our mother. Seeing that our world had just been flipped upside down, my grades were a direct reflection of my current circumstances. Once progress reports were released the school required me to sign up and attend mandatory after school tutoring to ensure I remained on grade level. To say that I was angry is an understatement. The only time that I looked forward to during the day and now they are requiring me to sit in this room with this man working on the subject I now despise. The goal was to complete all homework assignments there with him so we would have assistance with any problematic subjects. I sat in that room the entire time with a growing attitude with each day thinking about how I could be watching "Guiding Light" with Ms. Troy. This is not what I need right now. I get that math is important. I get that you must grasp certain concepts to prosper in this life but that, in that moment is not what I needed. I needed those bonding moments. I needed to be held. I needed to be reassured that life would not always be that way. The day our schools realize our students are faced with much more than reading, writing and arithmetic will be one to surely be celebrated. We must understand our children's needs and meet them where they are. Requiring all children to perform at the same standardized level without any regard for their day-to-day interactions is preposterous. I have never failed the state standardized test. I am not saying that I, or any other child in similar circumstances lacks the capability or should be held to lower expectations. What I am saying is that when you are in shit, Day in and day out it will begin to take a toll on you. It's hard enough for adults to leave their lives at the front door and conduct themselves accordingly once they reach their prospective workspaces. Why would we think children are any more equipped than the ladder? Anyway, I improved my grades enough to get through the fourth grade on time and in once piece, academically at least.

Now that the divorce was finalized daddy, Gerry and Christian were living in an apartment across fowler. They were no longer as close as I would have liked but daddy was always just a phone call away. There in that two-bedroom apartment, when we were all there over the weekend was equivalent to heaven, for me at least. We were free from the rest of the world, experienced comfort in knowing we did not have to hide our belongings and auntie Ari was right down the street. Auntie Ari is daddy's baby sister and his right hand. she was there for us when mama began to show her ass. She and her boys were the other half of our immediate family. With us being so close, figuratively speaking as well as physically, life was cool. On the weekends at least. We were good. It was the life I had been praying for every night we hit that corner at Mel's hotdogs. Just us and our daddy. No added drama. I was his partner in ensuring we were all on the up and up and I can honestly say that for two ½ days out of the week I was happy.

That summer, July 4th daddy woke us and informed us that we would be hosting a small family barbecue and he would be cooking so we needed to clean. No problem. We had no issues in doing as daddy asked us to. In the middle of our cleaning duties, daddy called all of us together and informed us that he had been dating someone and had invited her and her children over for the cookout so we could all get acquainted. Later that evening, they arrived. A dark-skinned woman and her three children. two boys and one girl entered my daddy's life and house and once again, nothing was ever the same. We had just begun to enjoy our simplistic life and here he goes adding these additional people. I know I have some nerves complaining about any additional persons being added to a family I was married into myself but if it were up to me, we had reached our maximum capacity. Oh well. He was an adult, and he called the shots. So be it. They arrived and socialized with everyone throughout the gathering. During conversation we realized we had previously met them at New Testament Missionary Baptist Church vacation bible school. They stayed the entire cookout and even spent the night. The next day they might have gone home for 1-2 nights. They returned with more clothes the following visit. I'm not sure what was up with their current living arrangements, but I kid you not, they came back to spend the night again, and a week later they were moving in. they were cool for what cool was. Her oldest was a year older than Gerry. Her middle child was a year older than me. Her youngest was the same age as Christian. But they were different. They Always seemed to have attitudes, stayed in trouble, and obviously didn't have that clear line of misbehavior that I have spoken of previously. They prided themselves in their rough and tough exteriors and enjoyed fighting. They did not mind cursing children nor adults and proclaimed they had issues with authority. As different as they were, they were our new step siblings. No, our parents were not yet married, it was years before that happened, but I guess when you make it to a certain age in life there is a different mindset on courting. The way they went about their affairs was like look, we are either doing this or we Ain't. So, they did it. Merging families for the second time was interesting to say the least. As problematic as my mother was and instrumental in her own self destruction and the dismantling of our previously established nuclear family, if nothing else she made me respect my daddy. We did encounter our bumps along the road in the first months of their relationship, however my mother took it upon herself to instill in me that this man, her man, and the man in our lives was my father and I was to respect him as such. I am sure this conversation was easier to have with me seeing that I was only 2 years old when they met, but it was one she was not willing to let go by the waist side. On the contrary, Ms. Celine was not so willing to ensure her children displayed any level of respect for the man who was now the head of the household they bombarded. From the beginning of their known relationship, they had no problem letting it be known that my daddy was not their father. They were blatantly defiant with any persons deemed "in charge", still they reserved a special level of disrespect and disregard for my father. They would often complain of his rules and high standards and refused to step up to the plate. Our life was simple, and daddy's rules were always clear and concise. Listen, work hard, be a team player, show respect and get good grades. Anything outside of that was working against the end goals. He wanted us to be great in all aspects of life. Following the rules would assist us in doing so. So, we did. Were we perfect? Of course not. Not only are we human, but we were also children. We broke rules sporadically, made less than perfect grades at times and displayed spoiled behaviors more often than not (okay maybe I am just speaking for myself). But we were never overtly ill-mannered or fresh. As a result, we were rarely in trouble and our close relationships among ourselves and with daddy kept us on the straight and narrow. Her children would often voice they did not appreciate that daddy had to continuously correct their behavior and actions and seldomly had to correct ours. Like bae, I am not in trouble. I do not conduct myself in manners which will result in trouble. Orjury beat my ass enough before we met y'all and I decided at an early age I do not like being in trouble. I do not like walking around with the nerves and guilt in anticipation of an ass whooping. I do not like the uncertainty of when it's coming. I do not like the feeling of disappointing my parents. So no, he does not speak to us as often pertaining to our behaviors. If you do not want him saying anything to you, tighten up. But of course, that would be too much like right.

When new chapters begin it is often easier to completely end and sever the previous chapters rather than dragging along the baggage into the future. That is how their new relationship and Ms. Celine's actions and comments made me feel. Like I was just the optional added baggage he continued to drag along. She, like the rest of the world, never grew to understand our relationship. I am not his child. He has no legal obligations to keep me around. He is not required, legally anyway, to bring me over to his home when he comes to get Taylor for the weekends. With his four children and the addition of her three there were now seven children in the home they were responsible for. That is a lot of mouths to feed, backs to clothes, clothes to wash and bodies to move. She seemed nice from the beginning. And she was nice enough, I guess. I was struggling with my own transition. For years I had been daddy's partner and the woman of the house so to speak. Although I was only in the fourth grade and Orjury had been there prior to these moments, she had forfeited her partnership with him long before. Now, here's this new woman who has stepped into our lives and taken over all my responsibilities and made it known that she is now the woman of this house. It was a difficult reality to deal with however I am a child so this is just now my reality. Hell, I am only 10 years old. Looks like I would be excited about being relieved of such responsibilities. And I was. I did breathe easy for all of 1 month. Following that initial month of their presence in our lives she began to voice her issues with my presence. When we are here for our time with our daddy and brothers, we were extra mouths to feed and clothes to wash. This was a job she did not sign up for and now doing so grudgingly. I overheard her and daddy having a conversation in the kitchen once about me possibly staying home and them only bringing Taylor over on the weekends. She did not understand the need for my presence. As nice as our relationship could have been and as long as they were together, our relationship was stunted right there in that moment. What do you mean I don't have to come over? Y'all just got here. If y'all would just go back to where you came from there would be more than enough room for everybody. You would not have to worry about whose clothes you are washing, and you could relax. The first thing I remember her making a big deal of was our towel usage. On the weekends we spend two nights and would obviously use washcloths and towels to shower. Her complaint was that adding our two washcloths and towels to the dryer required her to pay too much money at the laundromat for all the towels to dry completely. So, she informed me that while we were there visiting, we were not allowed to use our own towels. We were required to use Christian's washcloth and towel to not inconvenience her. That was cool with me. I am just here to see my daddy and brothers and as the "extra" child I don't have the right to have any feelings about it one way or the other. Remember, the goal is to not bring any added attention or unnecessary problems or drama for people to have additional reasoning to not want me around. Hell, you already do not want me here just because I am alive. I cannot give you any fuel to use against me. But do you know how that makes a child feel? To go from being overly loved and adored to now being placed in a position that sent the message that I am not worth the extra two dollars a week to dry some damn towels. Fucking eight dollars a month. It is not like she was washing our clothes. She had already made it clear that whatever dirty clothes we accumulated while we were there, we were to take them home and wash there.

Which was fine but now we cannot even have a towel. Every other child in this house holds enough value and stake in this home to wash their asses with their own towels. So, what does that say about me? What am I worth? Soon thereafter my menstrual cycle began and like every other girl it brought new considerations with everything. One weekend we were visiting, and I asked if I could get my own towel and washcloth because I did not want blood to get on the one I was to share with my siblings. Her answer was clear and cold. No. I was so hurt and embarrassed. I felt awful because as I washed myself and began to dry off there was blood. If only I could control it and make it stop my siblings would not have to be subjected to such filth. I decided at that moment, at the age of ten standing in the mirror in a pool of shame and tears, that just like my mother, she was not for me. She was for herself, her children and whatever benefits her. Once again, I am in this with the people who I know are for me. Mind you, there is nothing I could do differently other than accept this information as facts. She is not for my safety, my wellbeing, or my confidence. Hell, why would she be? My own mother refused to be these things for me. Following this incident, they began sending me to my god-mother's house every other weekend. Once again reiterating that my presence was a problem. Every other weekend they would be free from the responsibility of me. I was crushed. Daddy was willing to do whatever necessary to make her happy, even if that meant leaving me behind. When they began to travel it was concluded that there was not enough space for me, so they ensured those weekends I spent with God Mom. Like what do you mean there are not enough seats for me? Those are my family vacations you all are going on. Our family traditions with people you have just replaced me with, and I am not supposed to feel any way about it. I am not supposed to feel easily replaced. I am not supposed to feel abandoned. I am not supposed to feel hurt. I am supposed to just continue to smile, nod and agree and remember AT LEAST he does what he does for me.

Those every other weekend days lasted for about five months.

On the off weekend I spent time with whoever had time for me. Nanny worked on Saturday mornings up through the early afternoon cleaning houses as her side hustle. So, my days were split between auntie Arianna and God Mom. Nanny tried her hardest to set those days up to spend with David Pratt. A grown man I had no relationship with other than familial relations and a last name. Nine times out of ten he would call; say he was on the way and never show. Leaving me standing in nanny's house all day Saturday alone. My mother was off running the streets, my daddy was catering to the needs of his new family, David Pratt had followed through with his latest lie and I was just there. Existing. Being. Most times wishing, I was not. It sucks ass that I am stuck in these situations as the outside child raised by the masses being forced to endure this mental and emotional abuse because two immature adults couldn't grasp the concept of contraception. I did not ask to be here, and I promise in those moments I honestly wish that I weren't. I understand people only do the best that they can but most times we fail to consider how our actions affect our children.

Spending time with auntie Arianna and God Mom was always nice, however also interesting. My moments with them were flashbacks of what life used to be. During these times I felt important and loved. But now my life was different. First, being there meant I was not with my siblings which was never alright with me. Second, I was no longer the prissy princess they were raising me to be. I was only in the fifth grade but by then I had experienced real life. My mother was addicted to crack and not the hero I thought her to be. My grandmother was caring for me, but she acted as if she hated my daddy. I was experiencing crucial moments without the love and guidance of a mother and it showed. My hair was often a mess. My menstrual cycle began, and I was often on a hormonal emotional roller coaster and I was honestly over living. I often felt these two women lived in a rainbows and roses type of reality I was no longer privy to. They expected things to be nice and in order. At their homes we were to sit on the sofa a certain way, speak correctly, and conduct ourselves prim and properly. These things were not of great importance at that point in my life, but I made sure to conform and comply whenever in their presence. I had to learn how to get along, to get along. Being with them was never classified as my most comfortable moments though. They did not approve of our musical choices, did not approve of my choice attire, and found the way we spoke laughable. As much as I know they both loved me and were doing what they felt was best for me, me being my authentic self was not acceptable. In those moments they were looking for a young girl who believed in unicorns, loved pink, enjoyed wearing dresses and all things girly. I was and to this day am anything but. As I stated earlier, our parents took us to Freaknik. We listened to Uncle Luke. Like Mary J., I loved wearing combat boots and pink has never done a thing for me. I never liked dolls or the clean versions of songs. I dressed comfortably and despised anything frilly. I am not that girl. When you experience real life and all its traumas it's bound to change you. During our visits they were looking for a Naomi who no longer existed. Either way, I learned who they wanted and/or needed me to be and I attempted to conduct myself accordingly. It was not until later in life when I learned to be my authentic self regardless of other opinions that I understood how cool they are. The relationships we have currently are ones I would have never guessed we would experience. We laugh and talk and enjoy each other's company and it is mind boggling to me. Like, I wish we could have had this dynamic when I was younger, When I was missing my mother. I guess all things come with time and I was still a child so they could not act as my homegirl, but I could only imagine how this could have possibly impacted my life positively. Nevertheless, I get it. It was not their jobs to be Orjury. It was not their responsibility to carry on the mother/daughter dynamic she began with me. They could only be who they were, my aunt and godmother. True to themselves and living in a world Orjury free, lucky, and blessed.

The few times David Pratt showed up to "spend time with me" were worse than the days he stood me up. He would show up always in a rush and seemingly inebriated. Just as my mother struggled with her addiction to crack cocaine, my biological father wrestled with his alcohol dependency. At least that is what I always heard because we were never together long enough for me to find out on my own. Still, he attempted to prove their theory by showing up drunk every time I did see him. Although this was only a maximum of twice a year, it outlined a trend. He had two other daughters that I have known throughout my life and two I have only heard of. He spent most of my childhood in a relationship with Ms. Terry, the mother of his youngest daughter. She was a nice lady. She Had a family and home of her own and ensured they were taken care of. On the days he was supposed to be spending with me he would come pick me up, drive me straight to her house and drop me off with her children. He would just leave me there, in a strange place with people I barely knew. True, one of them was my sister but if we are being honest, I did not know her either. He would leave me there with them for twelve hours, return and ask if I had fun, and drop me back off at nanny's house. One hell of a way to spend time with your child. His daughter would spend those entire twelve hours bragging and boasting about being her daddy's little girl and proclaiming that he loved her more. It was always hilarious to me because nobody wanted her daddy. I was there against my will and me sharing their blood and last name was just the same. I hated being a Pratt. Every time I wrote my name it was a constant reminder of how much of an outside child I was. I was not a Jordan like my mother's maiden name and family. I am not a Walton like the people I have gotten through life with and grown closest to. I am not a Campbell like these extended people we have added to our familial ties. I am the only Pratt in all my circles, and it excluded me. It has served as a constant reminder that I am an outlier. It made me an option, not a requirement. From David Pratt I inherited his last name, lighter skin, and thick brown coils. Outside of that he has only been a thorn who shows up and pricks me sporadically. My mother had him placed on child support when I was one year old. According to her she gave him 365 days to prove that he did not need assistance in doing what he needed to do as a father. He failed and was presented with a child support order on my behalf. Now, just because it was ordered does not mean it was paid. I remember a six-month stint where the child support was paid. Outside of those months his support like his presence was few and far in between. Still, he and Ms. Terry treated me as the awful stepchild who took money out of their home. It is Not like it was supplied all the time but even if he was paying child support it's not like I went down to the courthouse personally and put him on papers. That is between you and the woman you decided to impregnate. Yet and still, he would call me well into my mid to late twenties asking me to call the child support office to take him off papers. By the time I made it to college he was so far in arrears there was no way he would be able to pay it back. Again, not my problem. If you would have held up your end of the bargain you would not be in this predicament. According to him, "you made it out of high school and on to college so it's not like you need it". How selfish and unthoughtful could one person be? It is true, I made it out of high school and on to college without any assistance from him. I made it despite him. Through the grace of my great God and the people who loved me enough to be there. Now that I am off and on my own, he wants to be set free from any ties binding him to me and of all responsibility. To him all I had ever been was a good nut in the woman who used to be bad one summer night in the eighties. I was not his daughter in need of help or his child who could benefit from the financial assistance. Hell, if I were receiving child support from him maybe I could have afforded to pay Ms. Celine the eight dollars a month to use my own damn towel. it is not like I have any say to when the state decides to relinquish you of your duties as a parent, but I was not about to put any efforts into that endeavor. He waited until I was good and grown, a two-time college graduate with a child of my own to want to build a relationship with me. After all those years of not being there, not showing up, not being responsible and not being a man, now he wants to be my child's grandparent. I was not in need of a daddy, I had one of those. However, I was supposed to be HIS responsibility and he failed to follow through. Now he insists on calling me so he can have a relationship with his grandchild. Sir, you can find the closest construction site and go and kick rocks with your socks off before you ever feel you have a right to a relationship with my child. If I'm feeling friendly, on a day when the weather is beautiful and bright, I might just extend an olive branch. I wish him no ill will and I harbor no bad feeling. I am just clear about where we stand. The arrogance in his demand to have access to my child is uncanny. You should have demanded to provide for me. You should have demanded to ensure my safety. You should have demanded to take time to get to know me. But you think demanding stories and photos so you can brag and boast about the child I conceived, carried, and had to bear is the way to go. It is a no for me. I will be back to you when I have time, in 30 years or so.

PANDEMONIUM

Middle school began and it came with new challenges, experiences, and accomplishments. Sligh middle school was not my first choice but it was the zone for nanny's house. I will never forget the first day of sixth grade. I walked onto campus and the first thought in my mind was, "oh I'm grown now'. I know, simply wrong and hilarious. I was all of eleven years old and I am not sure why I was in such a rush to be "grown" but that was definitely the feels. That year we wore uniforms, geography was my least favorite subject and I remember sitting in science class watching the 9/11 attacks. That year was also the first time I was confronted by one of my peers about my mother's extracurricular activities. We were all from the same neighborhood and since moving back to Nanny's house she had begun walking the streets daily and that bigger than life personality demanded attention. It was only a matter of time before someone noticed that I was the spitting image of the crackhead lady roaming the streets. I will never forget that conversation. An eighth grader asked me "how much will your mama charge to suck my meat?"

I was crushed. I hated her even more. She tarnished my reputation and name with her disregard for decent behaviors and there was no way I could deny I was her child. I was her from head to toe. From her big lips, no hips, thick thighs and knocked knees. The only thing she did not give me was her ass. That was just another way she showed her selfish trait. As a result of that conversation, I began to despise the mirror. She was the woman I harbored so much hatred for and I could not get away from her. No matter how many days she would leave and stay away, she was always right there staring me in the face. The older men in the neighborhood insisted on calling me little Orjury as I walked home from school which made me extremely uncomfortable. These men would gawk and gaze and make vile comments one should never say to a child. My defense was walking home as fast as possible without ever looking back or strolling with my peers. I also stopped looking in the mirror. For three years I would avoid eye contact with myself. Between our strikingly resembling looks and everyone constantly reminding me that I was her offspring, it was hard for me to differentiate between her and me. I would look in the mirror and be just as repulsed as if I were looking at her. I could not believe I could be so intertwined with someone who I despised. Those years she acted as a tyrant in Nanny's house, and everyone wondered why I became an overly emotional preteen. She would show up higher than a kite and upset about coming down. She would demand everyone to go to their rooms so she could lay on the sofa and watch law & order in peace. Just like she was paying the damn bills. The one hundred and twenty dollars she received from daddy every two weeks were inhaled just like any other dime she ever received. Not sure what she was getting from the old white man she was fucking in the living room on the couch while nanny went walking but she damn sure did not use it as a contribution to the house. Nanny being the peacekeeper she has always been, would instruct us to listen and do as our mother said. Just like it was not her house we were standing in. The home she purchased with my grandfather and worked hard to keep. I believe more than anything I have always struggled with how she disrespects my grandmother and she's the only one who has always had her back. On top of puberty, I was dealing with a mother who became a prostitute, a grandmother who did not understand why I refused to respect my mother and working through my feelings alone. I know everyone else has had to come to grips with their relationship with Orjury and how she has affected their lives, but she is my mother. She is where my life began. She has been a fucked-up daughter, sister and lover but imagine having that fucked up individual as your mother. Everyone else has had the opportunity to escape her. Her parents gave her away on her wedding day. When they divorced, her husband gave her back. Her siblings handled her at a distance and her friends were forced to cut ties. But where is the relief for her children? We were forced into this world through her and have been punished because of it ever since. My entire life I have been instructed to be the bigger person when it comes to my parents. The bible instructs us to honor thy mother and thy father. My opinion is that's until a certain extent. I just do not see honoring someone who could give two fucks about me. I believe the Lord instructed us to honor our mothers and fathers because most parents love and respect their kids, but that was not this.

Sixth grade was also the year they jumped my daddy. By this time, they had moved out of the apartment and into my daddy's childhood home. The house is on 34th and Deleuil. A 3-minute drive and ten-minute walk from nanny's house. With him being so close we were able to spend each evening with him until it was time to return home. Each afternoon following school I began walking to daddy's job and waiting with him until it was time to go home. This became our routine because according to Ms. Celine, Taylor and I were not allowed to have a key to their home. I was twenty-five years old before I received my first copy of the key, but I digress. Our routine was a way for us to have a few hours alone without being pestered with the needs and wants of others. Before his forced early retirement due to his disability, daddy was a teacher at a local alternative school. His class was composed of all the worst males within the school that no one else could handle. There were no females allowed in his room and his tactics were a little unconventional to say least. Nevertheless, they worked. These boys, who some had labeled societies worst held a level of respect for my father I thought only we would carry. They loved him. They were hell on wheels, but they typically did anything Walton asked. If not, the "old heads" in his class would ensure everyone stayed in line. I loved being there with him in the afternoon. There was something about watching my father receive the respect he was due. Being in a home with ungrateful minors who benefited in every way from his presences and yet insisted on disrespecting him never sat right with me. Their mother never demanded that respect and my daddy for some reason was too understanding for my liking. I guess that is what happens over time. After going through such traumatic experiences with my mother, at least this was not that, at least not yet. One day, I walked up to his school and one of his colleagues and closest friends greeted me and informed me that my father had called in sick. This was a pre cell phone era, for me, so I had to receive information conventionally. During my ten-minute walk to his home, I remember being overly concerned. "I wonder what's wrong?" "Poor daddy, he had to spend the day all alone". To know my daddy is to know that he is our baby. Between myself, my aunt, and my sister he has managed to be one spoiled rotten man. But that is okay with me. He is my daddy, and we take care of each other. As I entered the house I was dumbfounded. My daddy had clearly been in a physical altercation and I was crushed and confused. His face was swollen. His eyes were bloodshot red, and I could tell his spirit was hurting. I hugged him tightly and began to cry. After he helped me gather myself, we sat at the table and he filled me in on the events of the night prior to. We, Taylor, and I were there. We did not leave his house until after the sun went down and my daddy was fine when we departed. He informed me that not too long after we left his house, Mr. D'Angelo, Ms. Celine's ex-husband showed up and wanted to talk. That previous afternoon daddy picked us up from school. D'Angelo Jr., Ms. Celine's middle child and I attended Sligh together. When he picked us up, we reviewed the progress reports we both received that morning. If you re-member, one of daddy's simple rules was to get grades. Getting grades meant receiving reports consisting of A's and B's, maybe the occasional C. But D's and F's were a no go. D'Angelo Jr., also known as Dea pulled out a progress report displaying straight F's. During the seven and a half hours of school day and seven periods we at-tended for four weeks, his progress was 50% and below in every class. Naturally, my father informed him how disappointed he was in his grades. This message was conveyed with a raised voice, a few words of choice and a promised punishment. He insisted that we understood that just as they work to provide for each of us, it was our sole responsibility to work hard for our education. By this time, they had been living with my daddy for the past three years. It is not like he was a stranger. He was the man assisting his mother in caring for him and his siblings' needs. He was the father figure in their home, and they had no problem benefiting from that. They just did not want to live up to the heightened standards that came along with that privilege. During their conversation Dea became irate and ran out of the car towards his grandmother's house. From there he called his father to explain their interaction. His father later picked him up from his grandmothers to return him home, to my daddy's house. Once they arrived, he asked my daddy to step outside so they could have a discussion. During this conversation, their father expressed his disdain in my father chas-tising his son. The son my father was currently feeding, clothing, and exposing to finer things. Words were exchanged and Mr. D'Angelo threw a punch in frustration. They began to exchange blows and as my father was on top of theirs Deon, Ms. Celine's oldest son ran outside and attacked my father from behind. They jumped my daddy, in his front yard. They jumped him because he was not pleased with the poor effort his child had displayed the previous four weeks. How fucking ignorant could one man be? What is the message you are sending your son? It is okay to be a dumb ass and assault people when you lack the intelligence to express yourself verbally? Is that the lesson? Deon was put out of my daddy's house that night. At the age of 15, he was on his own. His mother begged my daddy not to put the rest of them out. Her oldest child and ex-husband had just attacked my father in front of his home, and she was concerned about her own security. If they were not on my shit list by then, they had just migrated to the top of that list.

Could you believe later that year they got married? They waited until my auntie Ari and our grandparents were out of town, and while we were all in school, they took themselves down to the courthouse and exchanged I do's. It was not like it was a spur of the moment occasion, her best friend made it all the way from Miami to Tampa for the ceremony. They knew what they were doing and did not care to share their moment with us. I always figured it was because they knew it was all full of shit. There was absolutely no reason they should have exchanged vows. They were too different. I know they say opposites attract but this was not the case. Their parenting methods did not mesh, at that point he harbored a hatred for her children and her undying alliance was to her destructive offspring. All those fairytale quotes about marriage were null and void in this union. You know things like present a united front, leave and cleave, the man is the head of the household, you lead, and I'll follow. None of that was witnessed in our home. They butted heads over everything concerning children, finances and at times religion. They were never on the same page, better yet they were never on the same team. In public they attempted to stand united, but it was all a facade. I have often wondered how they survived so long in that space, in that bed, between those sheets. It must be uncomfortable when you're sleeping with the enemy.

Seventh grade started off just as eventful. That first day of school I was called to the nurse's office and sent home within the first hour of being on campus. There were specific vaccinations required for students to receive before they could return to school and of course no one had taken the time out to ensure that I was compliant. Auntie Arianna arrived to pick me up from school. She spent the morning on the phone with Nanny and eventually drove me to a big brown building so I could receive the necessary vaccinations. Once we were inside, I learned that we were at the Hillsborough County Department of Health. From what I knew of this place, it was for persons without medical insurance or assigned physicians. So, what I learned from this experience was that I was one of those people. My siblings were all patients at USF physician's clinic. Dr. Shaw was their pediatrician. Daddy and Ms. Celine both had insurance and carried Taylor under their policies. They proclaimed they figured Nanny carried me on her medical insurance. Nanny had insurance but informed me that it would have been entirely too expensive to add me onto her policy. So, everyone else was worth the cost of healthcare. They were all worthy enough to ensure they had medical coverage. But of course, I was not so fortunate. I was just the byproduct of some summer fun, so my health and overall wellness was an afterthought. Hell, it was not thought of at all. I sat in that clinic and held back my tears of sadness, frustration and shame and thought to myself, "AT LEAST auntie cared enough to bring me here". The next week I was able to attend school. On that day we entered Sligh middle school and this time Christian and Aurora, also known as misty, were there too. It was their sixth-grade year and now there were four of us on campus. That day went off without a hitch, that is until the end. We were all standing outside in the car ride loop waiting on Ms. Celine to pick us up after school. Misty was standing talking with some friends and I approached her and asked her a question. She answered seemingly agitated and I responded by saying "okay heifer" and walked away. Back then heifer was a part of my everyday jargon. It was not said with any malice or spite. It was said with love, just as girlfriends refer to each other as bitch. Anyway, she was in front of friends and had to seem grand, so she turned around and responded, "Don't call me that again". So naturally I said "Okay heifer" in a playful manner. She turned around, charged me, and hit me there in front of everyone standing in the car ride loop. Of course, it was witnessed by someone in authority, and we were marched straight to the principal's office. I could not believe what had just taken place. One moment I was engaging in a simple conversation with my stepsister and the next I was in trouble for being in an "altercation" with her and explaining it to principle. This was not me or my life. I was not that type of child. Outside of my childish antics the first day of kindergarten, I was never in trouble at school. Now I was receiving three days of suspension because this girl needed to make a scene. We made it to my daddy's house and as we were being reprimanded Ms. Celine attacked me for being the cause of our suspension. I was wrong for calling her a heifer. A heifer is a young female cow, okay cool I get it. However, it is not like they, our parents had never heard me using that word before and if it was so wrong why didn't they correct my actions then? It was not until her child was in trouble because she couldn't control her raggedy ass aggression that I was wrong. What happened to "sticks and stones may break my bones, but words will never hurt you"? I was so over it and over them. There was nothing her children could do that resulted in her holding them accountable. Nevertheless, the days went by, I served my time, and we were back to our regularly scheduled programming. My entire life I had learned to be overly grateful for the immense love I did feel, even if that love hurt at times. In the seventh grade it dawned upon me that if it had not been for my extended family, I could have been in a rut rotting away and no one would have been there to save me. My daddy and siblings were the root of my love, confidence, and happiness. They were the Lord's love for me, manifested. In that actualization, I found tremendous guilt. Daddy lost his first wife, college sweetheart and mother to his children to medical complications in labor with Christian. He lost a partner; Gerry lost his mother and Christian unfortunately never had the pleasure of meeting her. I always claimed to be in the Lord's grace. He ensured I had what I needed to survive. But what about everyone else? What if she had to pass for daddy to be available for a relationship with my mother so he could be there to save me? That is beautiful for me but what about the people I love? In those same circumstances, now they were all subjected to the hell that is my mother all because God wanted to save me. If that was the case, was it even worth it? Why couldn't she have survived, and they lived out the life daddy envisioned for his children? In that grateful state was great pain. I was a seventh grader walking around with internalized blame of what was ultimately the inevitable. Life and all its unfortunate circumstances had nothing to do with me personally, but back then, that fact took me years to understand.

the year of 2003 marked the birth of Joness. Antwaniece, Markeisha and Kashisia were the three influential persons in this emergence. Witnessing them take off on any instructor who would dare mispronounce their names was awe inspiring. I was so jealous. We did not have the type of names teachers struggled pronouncing. Gerry, Naomi, Christian and Taylor. These names were standard, normal, and typical. I wanted one of those more ethnic names that I would have to over enunciate for people to learn how to say. I would stand in the mirror practicing how I would correct people for mispronouncing my name. Like, "Damn miss can you read"? I went home and explained this feeling to my family and my baby brother with his large imagination manufactured our ghetto names. Taquandra Dotestine Lafe Joness. Everyone in the family was granted a name, but mine stuck. Taquandra. T-A Q-U-A N-D R-A. I spelled it with so much attitude and tenacity. Over the years it became just Joness for short. Joness like Love Jones because everyone gotta Love Joness. Or Joness like Queen Joness because my brother placed me on a throne. I loved it. Being Joness replaced Naomi Pratt. It reduced the number of times I had to explain to people how I was the outside child. I am just Joness and at that point, that is all people needed to know.

That year I was also inducted into the national junior honor society. Academics had become a competition amongst myself and my friends. I thanked God for that piece of normalcy. For those moments I felt like a normal kid. We compared grades, completing assignments was a race and nothing was good enough if it was not an A. I believe that is also the year boys began to flirt with me. Mind you, at that time I had no clue that is what was going on. It seemed like everyone around me had begun dating and partaking in their dramatic play-play relationships. They were so overly concerned with the opposite sex. At that point, boys were aggravating and got on my last nerve. They were cute, but that was about it. They played too much, thought being dumb was lit and always seemed to want to pass licks. They would constantly hit me and run off laughing. In retrospect, I now understand those were love taps. But back then I was not on none of that. Keep your hands to yourself or I will throw an entire chair at you. Period. So, I kind of put a damper on the mood. It was around that time that I earned the nickname grandma. I am not sure how it started or who called me that first but from that point up until college, amongst my peers it stuck. It was so bad even my teachers began referring to me as grandma. I get it. I have an old soul, a southern accent and rarely hold punches when I speak. I referred to all my classmates as children and did not dress as promiscuous. By then I had not learned the beauty in my shape and tried to cover it in every way. I wore a long black sweater to school no matter the weather. I wish I could go back in time and snatch that thing off myself. There was no reason I should have been walking around while it was ninety degrees in a knee length jacket. However, I had not been fortunate enough to be introduced to Katt Williams and had recently discovered my first stretch mark. In my eyes it was hideous and thought if I kept it covered maybe it would just disappear. It was later in life, after my entire body seemingly became one large stretch mark that I stopped worrying about my stretch marks making a public appearance. Anyway, my style has always been centered around comfort. I am not a tomboy, but I am also not the girliest girl. There was no hair and makeup, I did not do nails, and I was alright with throwing on the first thing in reach after I woke up. Boy shorts, tennis shoes and t-shirt will always do. Especially since there was no one on campus I was trying to impress. They will get what they get. This attitude was always the root of a morning argument. Nanny wanted me to put more effort into my appearance and care more about how I presented myself to the world. We would have a routine morning debate the entire twelve minutes it took to arrive at the school. Her thought processes were so "old school", and she had a daughter running around on crack but was overly concerned with the clothes I put on my back. Ma'am, why are you so concerned with this, and not that? I would never dare to say such things to her, but I would display the attitude in my demeanor and on my face. Then feel guilty every afternoon for that uncontrollable attitude and call her job to apologize. I knew I was wrong for being so angry with her at times but experiencing such trauma and turmoil in those hormone raging years was dreadful. I guess the way I chose to dress was too on the borderline for their comfort, so it was something that needed to be addressed. One morning as auntie Arianna was taking me to a Delta Academy meeting, she began to ask me questions. She asked why I chose to dress that way and if I was having funny feelings about girls. She wanted to know if I was at least attracted to boys. I was attracted to them, but I was not sure if they were attracted to me. And again, they got on my nerves. This was her nice way of asking me if I was gay. The answer simply put, no. I am not gay. I love men and all things testosterones. Women are aggravating, hell at times I cannot stand myself. I cannot stand me, and my own emotional roller coaster and you think that is what attracts me? Hell Naw. I like men. Fast Forward fifteen years later, I birthed my first son, and she can't believe how handsome his father is.

That Christmas I remember receiving a few distinct gifts. Nanny bought me a necklace which I cherished. It was a basketball hoop. I did not play; I was just in love with the game. I also received a large boombox radio which I was overly in love with. Music has always been therapy and to have that new radio meant nanny understood that and helped provide me with that escape. After opening these gifts auntie Arianna handed me a bag with one of the largest smiles I have ever seen displayed on her face. My immediate thought was "oh this must be good". I opened it up and with great expectations I reached in and pulled out a book. A book. I was so confused. Why would she give me a book for Christmas? It was proof that we were not on the same page. She obviously did not get me. I would have never requested a book for Christmas. She saw my face, so she immediately knew my thoughts. She laughed and said, "I know, but just open it up and start reading, and you'll thank me later". I spent the rest of that break confused and left that book right in that bag, its rightful place. After Christmas breakfast with nanny and her side of the family we headed over to daddy's house. There we would open gifts, eat a second course of breakfast, and wait for the extended family to convene for evening festivities. After staying with daddy for the weekend we returned to nanny's house that Sunday afternoon. I was extremely excited to show daddy the boombox nanny got me for Christmas. I instructed him to wait outside in the car and I would bring it back out for him to see. I bolted inside to my room and directed my attention straight to the corner where I left my new radio. Of course, over my two-day departure my radio grew legs and magically walked right out of my room. I could not believe I had been so overly excited about my gift that I let my guard down. I knew better than that. It was foolish of me to leave anything of value in that house where my mother had free rein to poach anything without a pulse. Could you imagine how that feels? My mother had just stolen something that belonged to me and I was blaming myself. I was wrong for leaving it in the first place. But no, she was wrong for stealing it. I should have had the freedom to leave whatever, whenever and have the confidence that it would be there when I returned. I dropped my head and ran outside to tell daddy to go ahead home, there was nothing left to show. Mind you, at that point I had not even spoken to my mother to confirm that she took it. I did not need that confirmation or conversation for proof. Her past and our history was enough proof for me. Later that evening when she finally showed up, I had the opportunity to confront her about my property. Before she could get her high ass all the way through the door, I was on her. "Where is my radio"? She looked at me with her dumbfounded expression and crooked mouth. She began to speak ever so properly, as she does whenever she is high. "Oh, I let Randy use it because he said it was nice". Randy? Randy like our next-door neighbor Randy? What do you mean he thought it was nice? How in the hell did he know what my radio looked like in the first place? If you would have left it where you found it then he would not even have had the opportunity to like the damn thing. Her answer was dry and unconcerned, "I will get it from him tomorrow". The next morning, I sat outside for two hours waiting for Randy to show up. I approached this 20 something year old man and asked him for my radio. He looked me dead in my face, chuckled and said, "your mama sold that to me, that's my radio as of Christmas night". I was crushed. Then, I was pissed with myself for being crushed because I already knew what the deal was. She was not sorry or remorseful. She spent her days taking from everyone who ever loved her, and we were supposed to just forget and forgive because of our familial relations. Nanny told me to relax and not worry about it and she would get me another one soon enough. Of course, that day never came. At the end of the two weeks break I unpacked all my presents and began to prepare to return to school. In the process I saw that book and tossed it in my bookbag just for the heck of it. That first day back at school I sat in class bored and pulled the book out just out of sheer curiosity. I placed it on my desk and read the front cover. "The Coldest Winter Ever". The first line read, "I never liked Sister Soulja, straight up. She the type of female I'd like to cut in the face with my razor". From that first line until the last page, I was hooked. We were back in school and I was upset I wasted the entire break not reading the book. I was now in class rushing through assignments so I could open it up and get back to the story. As little as I conversed with my classmates before I opened that book, it was now even less. I did not have time for anything outside of diving deeper into that story. The setting, the characters, the realism, they were all so relatable. I remember sitting in class talking out loud to Winter just like she could hear me and being a disturbance during the lessons. I was so unconcerned about what was going on in those seventh-grade classrooms. There was a more exciting time going on between the covers of that book. I finished all three hundred and sixty-eight pages too quickly. I was disappointed to have to rejoin reality. The worst part about it was I had no one to have discussions with. So, I began to promote the book to my friends and let them borrow it while we were in class. This was my first experience with a "book club". We were just a group of thirteen-year-old girls enjoying the artistic stylings of Sister Soulja. Once word about the book spread there were fifteen or so girls all sitting around analyzing our readings. We criticized winter's decisions, grieved for the loss of her father's empire, and fantasized about who we would cast as Midnight in a motion picture. About one month later I was called into the principal's office. Once again, I do not make a habit of being in trouble, so I was completely taken aback once I was summoned. Once I arrived, she asked me if I oversaw the book club taking place in our seventh-grade classrooms. I smiled proudly and explained that I was not in charge per say, but it was my book, and I was allowing the other girls to read it as well. At that point I just knew she wanted to thank me. Not only was I being kind and sharing my gift with the world, but I was also encouraging her students to read, something the teachers get paid to do. Hell, I should have been on the payroll. She asked me if I had the book currently. I explained that I left it in the classroom for them to continue reading without me since I had already finished. She informed me that she would be coming to confiscate my book and calling my home for an adult to come and retrieve it from her office. She went on to expound on how not only was I reading inappropriate materials for someone of my age and maturity level, but I was also sharing such vile content with others. VILE? That was a good book and my auntie purchased it for me as a Christmas present. She was devastated and did not believe my auntie would gift such a literature to a seventh grader. She stated, "even if your family allows you access to such language and harsh themes, the other students did not receive permission to indulge in this book and their parents are not sending them to school every day to have you expose their children". I was so confused. Lady, if you walk these hallways and listen to these conversations this book should be the last of your worry. I am not exposing them to shit their parents have not already done. At least this time they are actively reading and expanding their literary catalog. I was dismissed from her office and let off with a warning. If any of my teachers were to see the book out in class again, I would be suspended, for promoting reading.

Freshman year was my first take at a senior year. It was 2004 and I attended George S. Middleton High School. That year was the first time since elementary school that I was back on campus with my big brother. Although he was a senior and therefore, we had no actual classes together, him being on campus gave me an extra level of comfort and confidence. I also had our god brothers Prince and AJ on campus. We acquired an array of additional siblings through our years of extracurricular activities. We had been participating in sports since 1994. Daddy was insistent on exposing us to as many opportunities as possible and allowing us to work at our niche. We tried baseball for a season and realized this was not our calling. From there was football, cheerleading, basketball, and track. The ladder became our familial sports. Daddy assisted in coaching every team we ever participated in. his strong presence and loving demeanor afforded us extra brothers. Brothers from all over the city, brothers from different backgrounds and from countless parents, but all brothers alike. So, my freshman year my three brothers were all seniors. This was a blessing and a curse. I walked onto campus the first day as an honorary senior. Every person I had any interaction with was a senior. I rode to campus with Gerry who was deep into his senioritis behaviors and not too concerned with making it to campus on time. This was okay for him.

He had completed all his high school credits. I, on the other hand, had just matriculated to high school and was starting off on the wrong foot. We arrived on campus late every day. Therefore, I missed half of the lesson for English 1 every morning. I was given a warning for my tardiness, and then assigned detention and in school suspension. So, we decided to miss the first period entirely. We would just arrive on campus for the second period rather than show up and be written up multiple times for tardiness. We would leave the house and drive around the city to waste time. Other days we would grab a blanket, arrive on campus, and lay down in the truck until lunch time, attend lunch and all afternoon courses. Again, I was a freshman, but I had developed an extreme case of senioritis myself. That fall we attended the homecoming dance, senior skip days and traveled with the summer track team every weekend as usual. I was also a member of the Hillsborough County Educational Talent Search. The ETS was an extracurricular group offering tutoring, community service and college tour opportunities for individuals maintaining a 2.5 grade point average or higher. In the spring of 2005, the ETS offered all members a spring break college tour in New Orleans and all surrounding areas. Somehow, I convinced nanny and daddy to allow me to attend the college tour. The trip was eight days long and consisted of 80 students from around the county. We took two charter busses to Louisiana and stayed on canal St. I had been to New Orleans multiple times with my family for the Bayou Classic by then, but this time was different. This time I was amongst my peers and without parental supervision. I did not have any close friends on the trip with me, so I was honestly on my own when we started out. I knew a good amount of the kids on the bus, but we were not best friends or anything. The bus ride up was cool. I sat with a childhood acquaintance for half of the trip. At a rest area he had a conversation with one of his male friends who informed him that he liked me. So, as we boarded the bus again, they switched seats. Mind you, this was a bus load full of hormonal, horny high school children traveling overnight. You can only imagine the touching and feeling taking place on this bus. I was totally unaware of their plan to swap seats, so I looked up and saw a big bright skinned boy stand-ing in the aisle cheesing from ear to ear. "Oh, you with me now". I rolled my eyes harder than I have ever rolled them before. His name was Walter and I had never met him prior to this encounter. We sat up and got acquainted for about an hour before he wanted to "get comfortable". I was not sure what he was thinking or who he thought I was, but I quickly informed him that whatever little girl he was looking for, I was not that. I do not play those games and you are not about to put your hands on me. We can lay here; we can share a cover. We can even lean on each other. But anything outside of that is a no go. Disappointed, he laid his head on my shoulder and went to sleep. Once we arrived, he shared with his friends how I was a boring riding partner. That was fine with me. I would rather be a boring riding partner than the trip hoe. We were only 15 years old. I had not even thought about being sexual or even had my first kiss. And he thought I was going to just let him take what he could get. Once we arrived at the hotel, I was spotted by a group of seniors who also attend Middleton. I did rec-ognize their faces, but we had never been formally introduced. One girl approached me and said, "You're Gerry Walton little sister right"? I replied with a quick "yes". She grabbed my arm and told me that I was staying with them for the week. On the agenda for the week was six college tours and one museum visit. Outside of that schedule we were on our own. So, I was the only freshman with a group of twelve seniors running around a city with a legal drinking age of 18. Every free moment we had, we spent on Bour-bon Street. We stayed up all night, they snuck me into the clubs and paid a man to hide me in his taxi when the authorities en-forced the city-wide curfew sweeping the streets. Then we would wake up the next morning as the walking dead to tour multiple college campuses. That week, I think we created the definition of a vibe. We were living young, wild, and free. They let me taste their drinks and still ensured we conducted ourselves responsibly. Whenever we would run into the chaperones enjoying their night out on the town the seniors would all crowd around me and in-struct me to duck down. I did get into trouble on one of the college tours. That afternoon we were all standing in a group at Loyola University. A boy was standing rather closely to me and kept shouting, "stop poking me". Completely confused, I would reply, "I have not touched you". A few moments later it would happen again, and he noticed a shiny pointy end protruding out of my drawstring bag. I had completely forgotten about what I had packed. Prior to my departure from my family, I understood that I would not have my daddy or siblings around for my protection. So, I packed Nanny's sewing sheers and intended on using them if anyone took me there. A chaperone witnessed me pull them out of my bag and confiscated them until we returned to Tampa. Till this day I still do not see the problem. If he had not been standing that close to me, he would not have gotten poked. The lesson from that encounter should have been for everyone to give me my six feet.

That year I also began my journey in the study of health sciences. Ms. Jordan was my teacher all four years of my tenure there. her courses were all prerequisites for one another and would end with a clinical rotation. Her courses and that classroom was my sole motivation for attending school. All the other courses were mandatory and what was necessary. Her class was voluntary and captured all my attention. In that space I realized my niche. In the past I had participated in sports. I was a cheerleader and competed in the race walk. However, I was never much of an athlete. Prior to high school I read gifted hands by Ben Carson and naively decided I would become a neurosurgeon just like he did. Freshman year I understood that career path was not my calling. At that point I was unaware of what it was exactly, but I knew I wanted to merge my new love of health science and knowledge of sport. I would spend the next fourteen years attempting to bring that dream into reality.

That summer I was required to attend summer school. All the days of lateness and skipping English caught up to me and I was charged with paying the cost. Monday through Thursday for six weeks I had to attend four hours of school for a language I could already speak. I was upset, but not receiving the necessary credits was not an option. I had to miss out on trips, stay home when my siblings were out on the town and go down in history as the only child having to ever attend summer school. Nevertheless, English is common sense. I finished the class, got the credit and was done with freshman year. Tenth grade was up next.

That year, my mother was incarcerated. Her charges of possession, drug paraphernalia, solicitation, and worthless checks caught up with her. Prior to then she had been arrested and held in jail several times. This time she was sentenced to prison. I was happy for her. If that is the only place, she could be saved from herself, that's where I would prefer her to be. If you're going to fight tooth and nail to end in that jail cell, I suggest they lock the gates and throw away the key. Nanny and Dr. Sims, Orjury's godfather, would both panic and attempt to scrape bond money together every time she was arrested. I never understood their goals. They would pay money to bail her out so she could return to the same environment and continue to run the streets. When she was out and free, she would disappear for days, sometimes months at a time before returning home. We would have no clue as to her whereabouts and nanny would be worried and concerned for her safety and wellbeing. The way I see it is, if yall leave her in jail at least you will know exactly where she is at all times. It may not be the best of environments or circumstances but when she is out, neither is where she chooses to spend her time. Anyway, this time there was no bailing her out. She was booked at Orient jail and sent up the road. I would frequently visit Hillsborough County Sheriff's Office inquiries online to view her records. As hurtful as it was, I would continue to do it. Like some sort of cruel and unusual self-inflicted punishment I unconsciously believed I deserved. Over the years her mug shots went from bad to worse. Her first mug shots were captured in the nineties and she resembled more of the woman I remembered. The further down her rap sheet I would scroll the worse off she had gotten. In ninety five percent of the photos, she was obviously high and the last one I remember she was overly inebriated. That was the first time she looked like an actual crackhead to me. She was sitting, had white ashy lips, bloodshot eyes, nappy hair, and a twisted mouth. By then I had known for years that my mother had an addiction. When speaking on it I would often say my mother "struggles with an addiction" or "she is addicted to crack". No, the woman in that last mugshot was a straight up crackhead. Nevertheless, as much as the photos hurt, they shipped her off and it was well with my soul. After being locked up for about one month she began calling and writing Taylor and I nonstop. We were receiving letters at least three times a week and phone calls almost every evening. Taylor and I had two totally different reactions. She was still a baby when I grew a deep unlinking for my mother. She was there in the trenches with us, but she had no recollection. Back then, she was just a little girl longing for her mother to be home more often and excited whenever she did have that interaction. She was excited to speak with her on the phone and happily replied to her letters. I, on the other hand, was. This is the same lady who would run the streets all day and go months at a time without coming to check on our livelihood when she was in the streets. But now that she was forced to sit her ass down somewhere, she wanted us to assist in her entertainment to maintain her sanity. Fuck no and fuck that. Nanny would force me to sit down at the table weekly to reply to my mother's letters. She would say things like, "no matter what she has done she is still your mother" or "come on sit down and write her a letter it will help her feel better". To be honest I was not a fan of helping her feel better. She showed me that she didn't give a damn about how I felt long before those moments and now I was supposed to bend over backwards to bring a daily smile to her face just because of the fucked-up choices she continued to make. The truth is, if she had not been in jail or prison, we still would not have been hearing from her in those moments. So, I was not about to be doing backflips for a bitch who gave me life and still had to be forced to check on my existence. I tried my hardest to explain my thoughts and feelings in the most respectful manner possible to nanny. I wanted her to understand my pain and how her disregard for my decisions added on to the gut-wrenching feeling. Again, there I was, being reared by someone who prioritized someone else over myself. It did not matter that I was hurting. It did not matter that she had destroyed life as I knew it for her own selfish pleasures. All because I was forced into this world through her womb, I was charged with being inevitably disregarded. If she benefited it did not matter how I was affected. So, I would sit there at Nanny's dining room table, writing a tear-stained letter feeling neglected. As disrespectful as Orjury was to nanny, I could not believe that nanny still prioritized her needs over mine. The message that sent me was, there was no one earth who would ever put me first. They all had someone else who would come before me. In my family, outside of my circle of siblings, I was a second-class citizen. As I aged, the reality of my needs not being prioritized was more understood. I am not her child, Orjury is. She was called by the Lord to love and protect Orjury during her tenure here. I was just an extension of that. And as much as she loves me, if there is ever a decision to be made between my mother and myself, there is no real competition. Anyway, the clock continued to wind down and she served her time. She was transferred to a work release program in St. Petersburg which was about forty-five minutes from where we stayed. Nanny completed the visitation paperwork and insisted on taking us to see her. Of course, I was livid. We were now spending our Saturdays crossing the bridge to see this woman. This was not how daddy wanted us to be raised. Visiting someone in prison. This shit was not cute. Being patted down, pushed, and prodded just to sit in a guarded room for two hours at a time to listen to her lies. Sitting in there selling dreams. She was clean at the time but that is not hard when the prison is in charge. She was saying things like, "It's going to be different this time" and "I'm going to stay strong for you all". I was not falling for the okey doke. This was not my first time being lied to by her and by then I had grown to know the lady like the back of my hand. Nanny was upset with me for not having more of an open mind and positive thought process about her recovery. I was just being realistic for my own sanity. I could not afford to get my hopes up for her to disappoint me again. If I just accept her faults as facts and her addiction as grim actualities, I could continue to hold on to the piece of sanity still in my possession. Those visits lasted for about three months before she was released. Could you believe she had the nerve to begin a relationship with another recovering addict while she was in there? During that time, she had secured a job at a realtor's office as an office manager. It was a good look for her. Like I have said before, when she is good, she is good. She had gained weight and was looking healthy. Her hair even seemed to come back to life. I guess that is what happens when you refrain from inhaling poison into your body daily. Anyway, she and her new man Andre were released at the same time and found a small apartment together in St. Pete. Daddy always said she needed to just find another addict to date because at least they would be able to understand one another. Even still, I thought they were such a cliche. How in the hell are you all going to keep each other straight when you cannot even keep yourselves on the straight and narrow? He was short, a recovering addict who had just been released from prison and he could not read. Orjury would get upset with me because I was not impressed. My internal thoughts, "Oh so we're just going to completely abandon all of our standards huh"? But hell, she had lowered the standards for herself, how dare she hold them for anyone else. She would read my thoughts in my facial expressions. One evening they drove into town to take Taylor and I out for dinner. This caused us to have to leave my daddy's house early so naturally, I went into that evening with a blatant attitude. They took us up to the pizza hut on the corner of 40th and Busch. As we were seated and began to order, Orjury ordered our usual, a meat lover pan pizza. Andre ordered something else and a side of jubilee peppers. The waitress was confused and asked a few times what he was referring to. He repeated three times, "jubilee" peppers. I glanced at the menu and said, "do you mean jalapeno peppers"? I laughed so damn hard at that table that night. No, she did not drag me from my daddy to come out and entertain a man ordering some damn jubilee peppers. She was mad. She told me how rude I was and how she was sick of me sticking my nose up at people. She then proceeded to compare Ms. Celine and Andre. She did not understand how I could show her respect and seem to care for her and not provide that level of love and attentiveness to her new man of the past two months. Truth be told, they could all kick rocks. Over the years I had grown a relationship with Ms. Celine, and we did have our moments but it's not like she was my person or my go to. With her and her family came added drama. Along with a relationship with her came jealousy from her angry ass daughter. I do love her but that came with years of turmoil within itself. The only reason she insisted on comparing the relationships was because while she had spent the past six years floating on her high, she had no clue what pain I had endured. She did not know who caused it or who if anyone had been there to comfort and mend it. All she cared about was comforting a man who she had just met in the pen.

Andre was from Jacksonville. Within a month of their release, they wanted to take a trip to go up and visit his family. Orjury insisted on dragging us along for the ride. I did not understand the need for us to take that trip with her. It made more sense for her to spend some time and get to know us again, but no. We had to travel with her, our recovering mother, and her recovering man. She had purchased a small bucket to get from point A to point B and across the bridge from time to time. This vehicle had no business going on a road trip. Still, they insisted. I was so confused with all the other adults in our lives. They all just let us go. At that time, they were acting like the court system. Just did not give a damn about our wellbeing. They act like they did not remember what this lady was capable of. Like they did not know she would voluntarily go missing. Or that they did not remember her leaving my daddy at the doctor's office and failing to return to get him. Or leaving us in the house when we were younger with no food in the kitchen. But because she had supposedly not smoked in those past few months it was okay for her to just take us down the road. Taylor was excited about the road trip. I on the other hand had spent that entire weekend nervous and on edge. I didn't know how much money she had, or what type of environment we were headed into, or if we would even make it back safely with that bucket of a car, we rode in. The house we stayed in was nice. His family seemed like good people. They cooked and laughed and danced and complimented my mother for being such a good woman. Of course, she got up there and put on a show like she was mother of the year. They had no clue that before that weekend we had not stayed under the same roof in almost two years. Nothing about that weekend was relaxing. I witnessed my mother talking to this man like he was a dog and drinking like a fish. Although alcohol was not her addiction it has never done her any justice. She cannot handle being intoxicated, no matter what the substance. I did not breath easily until she returned me to 3701. After three days of being with her I felt like I could finally exhale. If they were trying to create a nervous breakdown in a high school student, they were certainly heading in the right direction.

Before beginning the tenth grade I had to face one of the greatest Changes in my life. That spring Gerry graduated and was the first of our siblings to head off to college. We piled into daddy's dodge charger and headed to I-75 north, I-10 West. We arrived in Tallahassee, Fl at Florida Agricultural & Mechanical University and unpacked his items at Paddy Foote. I was overly excited for him. He was beginning the phase of life daddy had always been preparing us for. According to the adults in our family this would be the time we would develop our fondest memories. He had his books; we unpacked his room and took him for a last lunch before we hit the road. During that lunch I realized that I was too excited to be leaving him there. For the first time since I was three years old, I would have to learn how to survive life without my best friend. My big brother has been my confidant, my example, my first go to. If we leave him here that means I'm alone. I was immediately depressed. I could not fathom how I would ever survive. Mind you, we both had phones and it is not like we would never speak. But I would surely miss his presence. Once we arrived back on campus to say our goodbyes, I could not hold back my tears. I cried, hugged him, and ran to the car. Daddy and I cried from FAMUs campus and halfway back down I-10. This experience, as painful as it was, was the goal. He had survived our crazy life and high school and was now off on his own.

That fall, I returned to Middleton High School as a sophomore and felt totally alone. Because I spent the year prior to with seniors and seniors only, it was a new experience for me. I walked onto campus and had to get to know the class of 2008. In those classrooms were Chanelle and Terrell, my twin soul mates, a few of my classmates from middle school and a love one will only experience every blue moon. That year, sitting in Ms. Papineau's tenth grade English, I met my Jerome. He had just transferred to Middleton, so he and I were in the same predicament. I sat right behind him in class. I am not sure what sparked our first conversation but from that point forward it was never ending. Just like that, I met my best friend. He was a dark-skinned boy with a small frame and smile brighter than the sky. We held the same interest, took the same classes, and became attached at the hip. He was my sounding board, my right hand and go to. We spent all day together and each afternoon on the track with our adopted godfather, coach Dixon. That year, school was about one thing and one thing only, FCAT. tenth grade was the year we were all charged with passing each test to graduate high school. Every single class was designed around the topic of FCAT. Although others seemed to struggle with passing this standardized test, this was one problem I did not experience. Ms. Troy, that same fourth grade teacher taught me how to take that test and I invoked those same strategies until that last year. Geometry, on the other hand, became my nemesis. In that single year, sitting in Ms. Wolff's class I began to contemplate the meaning of life. I was doing awful in her class. I did not understand geometry, hated the concepts, and answered every question with a question. We were required to complete something called proofs. They actually sat us down and required us to prove that the objects they showed us were triangles. Like the fact that they all had three sides was not good enough. Or the fact that they, the teachers taught us that all three-sided objects were forever to be known as triangles was now nonexistent. Because I did not like the class, I did not do homework. It was pointless just like those dumb ass questions. They would ask us to measure the length of the shadow being illuminated from the tree standing in front of a light post. I would raise my hand and ask "why"? Who honestly gives a fuck about the length of the shadow? Nobody in the history of niggadom would walk past a tree and begin to measure the shadow so why are y'all asking us to do it? Each adult would reply, "well if you grow up and want to be an architect someday you will need to know how to complete concepts such as these". I was relieved. Well in that case this is an easy fix, I do not want to be an architect or an engineer. I explained to them from day one that I wanted to study sports medicine. That is why I went so hard in Ms. Jordan's class. So, since I know what I want to practice when I am older there is no need for me to have to complete these lessons. Or so I thought. That semester, daddy sat me down at his front table and cursed me out. "You don't have to like learning it and you don't have to understand why you have to learn it. You just must get the shit so you can get that damn diploma and move your ass on. If you do not ever use it again, that's cool. But learn it enough to get your ass out of school". I did enough to get the credit. Made it out of that class with a D. I felt depressed and ashamed. Yet again proving that I was less than.

By then Orjury had made her way back to Nanny's house. Never got the story on what happened but she returned, carless, jobless, single, and broke. Her coming back home threw her right back into her routine environment and just like that she was at it again. I'm sure that's what landed her back home in the first place, but at least when she was over there it wasn't right there in our face.

In December, Ms. Celine pulled me aside and informed me she had been planning a surprise sweet 16. I was ecstatic. It was 2005 and "My super sweet 16" was one of my weekly shows. She had already pulled together a few details and hired her best friend, auntie Rene, as the coordinator. For four months we planned and shopped and practiced with my royal court. The day we found my dress was nice but stressful. We picked a tiara, found my shoes and the dresses for the court. We drove all around town as we listened to misty gripe and moan about what she did not like about the event. Finally, Auntie Rene had to put her in her place and tell her it was not about her. I was so thankful that she was there. If she had not come to the rescue, Misty's mother never would have. We walked upstairs in a bridal boutique and there my dress stood on a mannequin in the middle of the floor. It was "My Dress". There is no secret, they spent a pretty penny on that evening for me. It truly was an evening to remember. My parents and grandparents proceeded to my court. I was escorted in on Mary J. by my high school crush and surrounded by love. As Daddy changed my tennis shoes into high heels there was not a dry eye in the building. We danced a waltz to Luther Vandross and took pictures galore. We stayed right up until midnight and daddy did not receive any of the receipts until later that night. That day was loved. I spent the morning in the salon and all afternoons being checked on. But that day, just like every other had its own dose of drama. Nanny was upset David Pratt had not received an invitation. I never understood her weird attachment and loyalty to him but that was not my business. If he wanted to attend a sweet sixteen for his daughter, maybe he should have thrown one like my daddy did. She suggested that he walk me in, or I split time in my father daughter dance to include him. I asked, "is he going to split the bill"? If not, he can sit down and watch me dance with my daddy like everyone else. She was upset, called me disrespectful and ended the conversation. Mind you, I had not seen David Pratt that year. Now she wanted him to have the opportunity to show up and be recognized like everyone else there who had been helping support me day in and day out. I eventually told him about it, of course he did not show. And just like Orjury getting locked up, that was alright with my soul.

One of my greatest gifts arrived right before I turned sixteen. His name is Deon Moore Jr., and he is the child I never knew I needed. In a very sadistic turn of events, the child who brought our family so much joy and love is the offspring of the boy who caused my father so much pain. Yet and still, he came into our lives and stole all our hearts. By that time, I had made up my mind to never have any children. After witnessing the sick love mothers carry for their children, I vowed to never become one. I did not want to love another human that much. After witnessing the interactions of Althea and her children and Celine and her three, I was convinced that motherhood was not for me. I did not want to lose all my common sense and defend wrong children until my death all because I was a mother. I figured if I could just be an auntie that would be enough for me. In February of 2006, a small brown skinned baby entered our home and cultivated his own space in my heart. Almost immediately, all those feelings I vowed to never experience were there. That baby boy was a love we all shared, but he was mine. From the time he arrived a mothering instinct was activated within me. Sacrifice for him was natural and meeting his needs were a priority for me. I'd made up my mind to just be the greatest auntie under the sun. My nephew's arrival that year allowed that dream to come to fruition.

Eleventh grade was a game changer. That year I received my results and confirmed that I was done with standardized testing for high school and by then I was driving. I completed drivers education sophomore year and received my permit. Driving daddy's suburban after he purchased his charger was a piece of freedom and independence, I never knew I needed. I was not going anywhere fancy or particular. I mostly ran errands the adult no longer had to. Still, it was great. It gave me that "I'm grown" feeling all over again. I began to go out with more friends and realized there was a countdown until my departure. I only had two more years to survive in this environment and I would be off on my own. By this time, I was active in Delta Gems and would spend many weekends completing community service projects with them. We had monthly meetings and attended statewide seminars. Being home and so involved with sports we were always surrounded by boys. Delta Gems was my opportunity to learn how to interact with girls my age. At home there were three of us girls, but I was Taylor's mother and misty never allowed me to be her sister. So, it was with the Delta Gems that I learned to enjoy the company of girls.

At these events We clowned and joked and got split up for being "bullies". I was able to let my hair down and be a kid. None of them knew my mother and that helped maintain my peace. They did not pity me or attempt to shame me like the boy in middle school did. I was just one of the girls, getting grades, building a resume, and trying to be great. As a junior I completed all the remaining required credits outside of economics and English IV. From an academic standpoint junior year was not fun at all. There was chemistry, algebra II and two health science courses which were Hella demanding. However, it did cultivate an environment which allowed me to be academically stress-free senior year. I worked hard junior year with Donovan right by my side. We held each other accountable and supported each other socially. He quickly became a part of my family and loved just the same. He traveled with us to track meets on the weekends and had to run errands just like one of the kids. Together we conquered the eleventh grade and made plans for our bright future.

William Davis Jordon is my mother's father. Before Orjury met my daddy, He was my man. He was my grandfather, confidant, person of choice and friend. Lil' grandaddy is what we affectionately called him. He earned this name because of his smaller stature in comparison to granddaddy Walton. Lil Granddaddy was my heart, and I was his. He lived in west Tampa in a small duplex, drove a white thunderbird car and spoiled me rotten. In preschool I was enrolled in JMARS Christian academy at Cathedral of Faith Church of God in Christ. One thing about me that has never changed is my picky palate. I despised every dish they served at that establishment. Being the loving retired grandfather he was, my grandaddy would show up to the school each afternoon on time and bring me something to eat for lunch.it was typically a lunchables. He would then return two hours later to pick me up from school. I would spend each evening with him at his brother's auto repair shop. When I think of simpler times those were some of my happier moments. The nostalgic feelings of smelling propane gas and smoke, eating Lunchables and getting his car door caught on the curb. He lived alone when I was younger. My grandparents were divorced before I was born but they were both always heavily present in my life. Not sure what year it was but I guess I was in the second grade when grandaddy had his first stroke. As a child I had no clue of what that was or what it meant. All I knew was He was getting older and could no longer live on his own. As a result, granddaddy moved in with us. As a family we cared for him. We fixed his plate and made sure he was bathed. His presence always added an extra level of comfort during the chaotic days. It was not too long after that his health took a turn for the worst and he had to move into a nursing home. I hated that place. The entire building smelled like pee and once he got there, he acted like he did not know me. He insisted on calling me Orjury. It took me a long while to realize just how sick he was and just how much I resembled my mother. He stayed there for a few years before he passed when I was eleven.

In the summer of my junior year, Lil granddaddy's children all received a settlement from suing the nursing home for negligence. The four of my grandparents' children and the daughter he produced outside of their marriage. They all received a lump sum of cash. Somewhere close to eighty thousand dollars to be exact. Of course, we had no clue as to what was going on. You know with the whole keeping children out of grown folks' business. So, we arrived home one evening to gather our clothes to take with us to daddies for the weekend. As we went into the house, we were greeted by Orjury and five of her most peculiar friends. I will just say that instead of calling them all crackheads. They all seemed to be high out of their minds and nanny was nowhere in sight. I instructed Taylor to gather her things expeditiously. As we hurried to get out of the house Orjury stopped us in the hall and pulled out a large wad of cash. She handed us each a one-hundred-dollar bill and told us to have a nice weekend. I took it of course and darted out of the door. It was obvious to me they had stolen that money and were in the middle of celebrating. It was not until that Sunday evening when we returned that we learned that money came from their settlement. That was the summer or 2007. That day, when our mother gave us two hundred dollars in total, was the last time we laid eyes on her until January of 2008. She gave nanny ten thousand dollars as an agreement she had with her siblings and left. She still had over seventy thousand dollars in her possession, and she just left us. In those months she did not stop by. She did not call. She had not been arrested. She had not developed a case of amnesia and suddenly forgotten the address. She just left us. To be quite honest, that was such a peaceful time. She was not there to cause hell or yell. She was not there to take from us each day. We were given a window of bliss. Still, it showed how raggedy she was. She had just been gifted thousands of dollars and she abandoned us once again. I began my senior year without a clue about my mother's whereabouts. It was not until January of 2008 when Nanny showed up one evening to pick us up. She crossed Hillsborough avenue headed in the opposite direction from our home. I asked where we were going and she replied, "we will be there soon". We got in that car and took a three-minute drive across one main road and pulled up to a small ugly green colored house. As we pulled up my mother came out. As Taylor hopped out elated, I sat there once again pissed. This bitch been gone for over half a year and aint even checked on us and she has been three minutes down the street this entire time? Take me home. Nanny explained that they ran into each other at the grocery store that morning and Orjury gave her the address to bring us by. Just like she had not known where we were or who we were with or how she could have gotten in touch with us. She took her money and had been living with some new man for the past seven months spoiling him and fixing up his home. If this lady was not the definition of a raggedy bitch, I didn't know who was. I finally walked in with a chip on my shoulder and an attitude to match. It smelled like a mixture of smoke and crack. I could not believe they were excited to see her. Like she brought value to our lives. She had always valued herself and her high over us all, and now it was this new man. She bragged and boasted how she had gotten his roof redone and the walls freshly painted. How dare she stand in our faces and run down a list of things she financed for someone she did not push out of her uterus. She had not financed shit for us since I was in the third grade, and as soon as she could again, she ran away. We left that evening and once again nanny did not understand my take on the circumstances.

I had sunk into a dark place in that chapter in my life. To be perfectly honest I had to pray my way out of it and that was not until about a year later. I liked being angry with her. Her actions further fueled my hatred and justified how vile my visions of her had gotten. I verbalized my wish for her demise. "If you have all of that money looks like you would just go ahead and overdose". She spent so many years taking from everyone who ever loved her just to afford that cheap ass high one rock at a time. Now that she was sitting on money, she wanted to practice some self-control. No girl! Go smoke to your heart's desire. Now that you can afford it, go all out. Smoke until you cannot smoke anymore. As awful as it was, I wished for my mother to die. If she were no longer here, we wouldn't have to worry about her whereabouts or health. We would not experience distress whenever she did decide to be present. We could mourn, get it over with and move on. I have been slowly grieving the loss of my mother since the early nineties. I was just hoping to close that chapter of my life and put it all behind me. These were my honest thoughts and feelings throughout senior year.

Nanny decided to purchase a gold Nissan Altima for me prior to senior year. It was ten times smaller than the suburban that I learned to drive in, but I learned to love it. It was clean, had great gas mileage and more importantly provided me with a means of escape. I was no longer at the liberty of everyone else's schedule or feelings. I drove to school, to my scheduled clinicals and all social outings. Each morning I would stop by the twin's house and pick them up on the way to school. Mind you, being totally defiant. When Nanny gave me the keys, she made it perfectly clear I was to have no one, at any time, ride in my car. Of course, I responded with a yes ma'am and went on about my business. Donovan was with me 24/7 and that was not going to change. Plus, I did not see the point in me having a vehicle, living in the same neighborhood as my best friends and not stopping by to get them on my way in. So, I did, Every morning. One morning there was a bad accident heading towards campus. Nanny explained to me a specific route to take to avoid the commotion and make it to campus on time. I nodded my head and walked out. I could not go the way she explained because the twins lived in the opposite direction. As I drove down 36th St. A man pulled out in front of me running a stop sign and totaled my vehicle on the corner of 36th and Deleuil. Just like that, my taste of freedom was over. That was my first experience in doing the exact opposite of what I was told and having to pay a major consequence. The second and final time was later in college.   Since Orjury invited us back into her life I began calling her everyday needing a few dollars. She caught on and had a temper tantrum saying I was only using her for her money. Duh. what else was I supposed to call on her for? Love, time, compassion, empathy? Nah., she had already proven she did not have those things for me so I figured I would just get what I could get. It did not last too long. Apparently it only takes one roof, a few coats of paint and eleven months to smoke seventy thousand dollars away. Eleven months later she was back at home. She was broke, angry, and once again could not afford to get high. This time her level of meanness was unfathomable. She took over the front room and we were all supposed to stay in our rooms whenever we were home because she was miserable. A position she put herself in, once again. She had plans on marrying the man. He had cancer in every fiber of his being and did not have long to live. She moved herself in and made herself comfortable. She spent those months in his home plotting on inheriting his property after his inevitable demise. During that time, she treated his grown daughters like shit, then appeared surprised after they put her out of their father's home immediately following his sudden albeit expected passing. That was nothing but her acting skills rearing their nasty head again.

That spring I felt as if I was floating on cloud nine. I had finally matriculated through my health science courses and was able to begin the senior clinical rotation. Although I was enrolled in a full course load, the only courses which were required and of grave importance included English IV and clinicals. The remaining five courses were attended randomly and at will. I would however garner permission from the instructors to miss the class meeting. Donovan and I spent two thirds of our day with Coach Dixon. Then we would leave campus together and pick-up lunch on the way to our clinical assignments. We completed our assignments at a local nursing home and eventually graduated to St. Joseph's Hospital. We learned so much from Ms. Jordan. She was not the youngest or hippest teacher. What she was consistent, strong, understanding, and knowledgeable. She was exactly who we needed. She got to know us, held us accountable and required more of us than we knew we could produce. She would constantly tease Donovan and I for not dating. She could not grasp the concept of us being best friends. Because we were attached at the hip, she said she would rather us recognize our love and avoid searching for it in others. She warned us that if we did not choose to be together during those years, we would one day marry other individuals, produce families, realize we were meant to be and eventually end up with each other. Her parting words right before graduation, "Don't forget my invite to the wedding". I thought she was hilarious. We did not see each other like that. I have never considered him a cousin or a brother, but my best friend. He was family. He was the first man who valued my soul outside of my household. It was no doubt about it and no denying it. We loved each other. As a matter of fact, we all loved him. My daddy would even let us stay at his home unsupervised. According to my daddy, that only took place because he trusted Donovan. He held that much respect.

One week prior to graduation, sitting in Ms. Jordan's class we were all sharing our plans for the near future and wishing each other well. By then, Auntie Arianna and I had completed our application season and I had decided to attend The Great Bethune Cookman University. It had not dawned upon me that I would have to learn to get through life without my best friend. That afternoon, after sharing my life plans with the class Ms. Jordan stood up to congratulate Donovan on enlisting into the armed forces. My eyes became fixated on him. "The What"? I could not believe him. First, he made this decision that I did not fully support. Second, he made the decision and followed through with enlisting without speaking a word. Thirdly, he was informing others before even hinting at anything with me. So, were we not as close as I understood us to be? Were we going to graduate and go our separate ways permanently? It was all so confusing. He finally spoke and explained that he was trying to find the right way to tell me. He knew that I would be worried about his safety and not overly enthusiastic about his choice, so he decided to keep it to himself (& everyone else) until the time was right.

We graduated on May 28, 2008, 3:00pm at the University of South Florida's SunDome. I completed high school with a 2.95 GPA. I was right on the brink of a 3.0 which was the standard for the students who were deemed academically successful and noteworthy. With my documented GPA I did not qualify for any scholarships nor was I prestigiously acclaimed. I kind of just finished high school. With all that I had been through you would think that my high school diploma would be valued more than that. Instead, it felt like everyone was saying, "Well you made it, but you're not quite good enough". That was fine. My diploma and measly 2.95 GPA were priceless to me.

FREE JONESS

Graduation was my first step towards freedom. My opportunity to escape the current hellhole I had become accustomed to and go experience joy for the first time. A life without immense fear every night. A lifetime full of 24/7 anxiety would finally come to an immediate halt. I worked just well enough to earn a seat at Bethune Cookman University. In the summer of 2008, I attended freshman orientation for an informational binge and to become accustomed to the campus. Nanny, Auntie Arianna, and my mother accompanied me. I stayed in Joyner hall and enjoyed the entire weekend. Outside of Orjury walking around campus putting on a show and harboring attention it was pleasant. She insisted on conversing with the other parents and bragging about how much she did to get me there and how much of a struggle my high school journey had been. If anyone in this world knows how to get under my skin and on my last nerve, it would be her. This lady had not done shit for me and she had the nerve to walk around with the gumption to brag on me. I understand that we, her children, were the last great thing she accomplished but do not come in here taking my joy with your antics. Just let me be. She also caused a scene with auntie and nanny because she insisted on smoking in nanny's car because "she's grown" and she "needed it". My entire life she would assert her claim on her level of "growness" and inform others of what she will and will not do because of it. She threatened to act an ass if she could not smoke in my grandmother's car. How in the hell are you going to demand others to be uncomfortable in the space they finance? My grandmother is not a smoker and like the rest of us did not want her possessions to reek of that awful stench. But unfortunately, she has a daughter named Orjury who is alright with everyone else's misery at her mercy. And I mean any and everyone, especially her mother. That weekend I attended the information sessions, one or two parties and made various connections. One of these connections became my very first boyfriend. He was a six-foot, brown skinned stocky football player. He had recently added me into the myspace (I know right) group of incoming freshmen. He was from Los Angeles and decided to come to Daytona Beach to join the football team. He was Hella sweet, attentive, and intentional. He let it be known that he liked me and wanted me to be his girlfriend. It was new for me, but I honestly liked it. It had not been more than twenty-four hours on that campus, and I was already defying all the advice we received the day prior to. Each upperclassman we encountered on campus gave two consistent pieces of advice. The first piece of advice was to frequent the library as often as possible. They all explained that the keys to success were in the library and there would be no getting around that fact. They were seemingly begging us to begin our college careers on the right track and not wait until it is too late in our years. This advice mirrored something daddy had been saying our entire lives. He always said if he could go back and do college again the one thing, he would change would be to study one extra hour a day. So, this was advice I was mentally prepared to adhere. The second piece of that advice was to avoid relationships at all costs. "They are only distractions; you will not be able to focus on the goal at hand". Me with my combative teenage spirit insisted on defying the odds. In my I'm every woman moment I just knew it could begin a relationship, mind you the first one of my life, begin college, and maintain a 3.0 average. Mind you I had already proved that the 3.0 was a challenge, in high school. Now I was going to add a teenage, emotional rollercoaster of a relationship to the mix and be invincible. Just foolish and naive. But hey, I am Every Woman, right? So, we spent time together on campus as much as we could before it was time to depart. By then we had exchanged information and proclaimed ourselves a couple. We would be apart for just a few weeks before we were reunited where it began. I returned home with five weeks to prepare for my departure. In that time, I had to find a computer, purchase all purple decor for my dorm including my hangers, and say the final goodbyes to all my loved ones. It had not dawned upon me that for me to go and experience joy and freedom, I had to leave all the people who made me feel free. I met with Donovan and we said our final goodbyes before he left the city for bootcamp. It was a tear-filled experience, but I knew it was only a matter of time before we would be together again, so I was already counting down the days. By then I had realized I would be able to benefit from his military discount, so this poor decision had grown on me. He said that thought process was selfish and self-centered. That is funny because that's exactly how I felt about his decision to enlist, so we were even. The morning of my departure we packed up at nanny's house. Nanny, auntie Arianna and her good friend Ms. Debbie, Orjury, and Taylor loaded into two vehicles to take me back to Daytona Beach. Before we could leave our neighborhood, we had to make a quick detour so I could say goodbye to my brother and daddy. It was early in the morning, so Lloyd was still half asleep, but he did come outside to embrace me. For so long, he served as my confidence in human form so venturing into this next chapter in my life without him required me to develop a new level of personal strength. At an early age he began referring to me as the queen and eventually made me believe it. Because we were together at every event and practically joined at the hip there was not an arena I stepped into without that extra boost of confidence. Now, here we were fifteen years later, going our separate ways and I just was not okay. We eventually gathered enough strength to let each other go as I turned and looked at my daddy in his tear-stained face. This moment was harder than him divorcing my mother or us leaving Gerry on the hill. He would not be simply across fletcher or in the same neighborhood four minutes away. For the first time in history, I would reside in a separate city than my father, my confidant and caregiver. We embraced so long everyone in the vehicles seemed to get aggravated. We were forced to let each other go because we had a schedule to keep. I got back into the truck and wept halfway down I-4. in the vehicle I was questioned about why it hurt so much to leave him. If they only knew our story. If they knew how he has kept me and been there to protect me. He even shielded me from the woman who was assigned by God to care for me. In that vehicle, as we drove 140 miles east, as hurtful as it was, for the first time I felt like I could breathe.

Once we arrived on campus it was not an easy transition. There was a series of lines and waiting. Followed by a stent of waiting in more lines. We visited a line for housing and financial aid, I received my previously conceived schedule and finally picked up a set of dorm room keys. At 3:30pm I entered Joyner Hall on the corner of Mary McLeod Bethune Blvd, room 319A. There were four girls assigned to one room and three rooms to every one bathroom. The room was tiny, we were big, there were bunk beds and we had entirely too much shit. In all of that, I was in heaven. I was overly excited to be in there, a space I would not have to share with my mother. I was done hiding items and falling asleep in fear. I could rest easily knowing I would not have to walk on eggshells around the angry intoxicated lady. We began to unpack my belongings and label each area. They all elicited their interior design genes to create the look. I was happy they were there because that is that creative girly thing, I didn't have in me. Three hours later we had completed the task at hand, and it was time for them to head back to Tampa Florida. They, my family had successfully gotten me, the community child, off and into college. We began our formal goodbyes, and they were quick and to the point. That is until I reached my sister. Taylor grabbed my neck and squeezed too tight. She whispered in my ear, "Come back with me". As I cried, I explained that I had to stay. She was in the eighth grade, so she understood the natural order of life. She just did not want to be left in that home to survive them alone. She was my baby. Taylor is my first child. The last one my mother carried and gave to me voluntarily. It was cruel of me to leave her alone. I experienced heartache and internalized all the turmoil, but at least I always had her with me in the trenches. I finally reached my opportunity to escape and had to leave her behind. She cried hysterically and begged and pleaded with me. She had just finished utilizing all her creativity to ensure my setup was pretty and then did not want me to stay. Once again, they had to end our farewells and pry us apart. They walked outside and I watched from my third-floor window as they got into their cars.

I waved until they were no longer in sight, and for the first time in fifteen years, I exhaled.

Once they left, I took the opportunity to get acquainted with my three roommates. We were in tight living quarters and I typically would never voluntarily interact with so much estrogen, but our mix worked. Sharee of Naples, Niecy from Miami and Amanda ventured all the way from Chicago. We were all different, but we all harbored old souls. We enjoyed dry humor and bonded over old episodes of Golden Girls. In that room we told each other the truth and showed love like we thought one's family would do.

That first week on campus was about business for me. If you re-member I graduated from high school with a 2.95 GPA and was unfortunately waitlisted from my first choice. I wanted to attend FAMU. My brother was there, they had my major and I felt I would be more comfortable ultimately. Because I was waitlisted, I ended up at Bethune. Nanny and auntie Arianna expressed I needed to be there to "become my own person" and "spread my wings". At that time, I did not understand or agree. I went to school with the sole intention to garner an acceptable GPA so I could transfer to the correct university. I planned on completing one year on campus so I could transfer. I was focused on that one goal. Evan had decided to stay in California until the spring, so I did not have that specific distraction. That first week I found my classes, purchased all my books, and began to read ahead. I was on a mission to be great. In high school I had all the problems in the world surrounding me daily. This success or failure would be on me. I created a schedule and held myself to it. I outlined times for studying, assignments, and even writing Donovan. I was so focused I was surprising myself. That lasted for all of three weeks.

It was easy to make friends and acquaintances. The administration at the university created our first semester schedules and separated us into what they called learning communities. There were eighteen of us who shared the exact same schedule. This enabled us to become well acquainted and accountable for one another rather quickly. We learned everyone's academic strengths and weaknesses, study habits and sleeping patterns. We all visited the cafe together and helped each other feel a sense of belonging. Our group was exceptionally diverse. The immaculate eighteen consisted of athletes, band geeks, math geniuses and fraternity groupies. Our bonds grew from class assignments to study sessions and eventually all-night parties. We shared dreams, current crushes, and deepest fears. We became family instantly. I even shard them with mine.

On campus I had six upperclassman male cousins. They were all from Tampa and shared a house off campus. That first year, they took me under their wings and taught me the ropes. They covered topics like what classes to take, professors to avoid, books to purchase and parties to attend. They were my saving grace while at Cookman. They were my first form of transportation, first line of defense and constant entertainment. My first individual shopping trip I was accompanied by Van. Upon checking out he was dumbfounded to learn I spent 156 dollars. As we loaded his vehicle with my personal items for the dorm, he yelled at me and explained that I had to start thinking like a broke college student. "You don't have money to be shopping like that". "The next time we come to the store, you shop, and I'll check you out". That was fine with me. I was not sure what him checking out would change if I am still shopping the same way, but I was willing to oblige. Two weeks later we returned to the only Walmart in Volusia county. I walked through each aisle just as I did the weeks prior to. Van greeted me at the front of the store with a large smile and said, "aight, you done"? I confirmed and handed him my full shopping cart. He giggled and pushed it into the self-checkout line. As he began to swipe each item, I noticed he would swipe one item and place five into a bag, swipe one item and place another five in a bag until the cart was empty. I was overcome with nerves. "Van, what are you doing"? As my hands began to shake uncontrollably. "You either going to stop shaking or go sit in the car, relax". I tried my damndest to keep my hands still in my pockets as we walked out and loaded the bags into his trunk once again. We climbed into the front seat and he handed me the receipt. I spent thirty dollars on the same number of items as the first shopping trip. He chuckled and said, "Your Welcome". I felt awful. It was not like I was the average broke college kid. I had money at that point of my college career. Nanny had been saving my entire life for my college fund. It was not like I was rich and to this day I am still not sure how much money was in that account. I was honestly running through money frivolously. I had overdrafts every two days, did not understand how to work my online banking and was not abiding by a budget to save my life. All I knew was when I needed more money, nanny would transfer more into the checking. But at least with Van doing my shopping the dollars would stretch a little further.

I was a frequent visitor at their off-campus house. I was a part of the cleanup crew for their recurring house parties, would miss curfew to spend the night on a regular basis and was a witness to random acts of drama. There, I encountered girlfriends scratching their cars, domestic arguments, and disputes. My focus turned from books to social in one simple conversation with my cousins. One evening I was scheduled to study biology before bed. They called and invited me over for an evening of spades. I did not even know how to play. They insisted that I attend and vowed to teach me the game and all their tricks. I easily caved and that was all she wrote. We stayed up until the break of dawn on that card table. The next day I missed class, talked with Evan on the phone all day long and called Van to say, "aye let's do that again". Just like that, I morphed into a true college student. I made a deal with my resident assistant, Camille. If I'm not here, I'm with my cousins. Since she was close with them, she knew I was safe. I missed the 11pm curfew more times than I made it. She only required me to check in with her once a week, so she knew I was still breathing. Bet. That was a good deal. Every evening she would mark that I was there, and I would check in with her on Wednesday afternoon.

That was the beginning of the greatest stents of my dumb decisions.

I began sitting up all night on the phone with Evan. He was still in L.A., so he was three hours behind in the Pacific Standard Time zone. We would talk all night and text all day. On the days I attempted to go to sleep on time it was never a success. I had 8am biology with Dr. Sin. I needed to get to sleep well before 2am so I could be a productive student. Every night around ten I would attempt to hang up on him. "Come on bae, it's on seven 'clock here, if you hang up, I won't have anyone to talk to". "You'll get mad if I start using that time to talk to another girl so just stay up and talk to me". Like a fool I agreed to stay up and keep him company. That was the first example of how I was dating my greatest distraction. We would talk, argue, and cry. At the end of the conversation, it would be midnight his time and 3am here. By that time, he would insist we get some sleep so I could make it to class the next morning. That was a joke. I made up my mind about not going to class about two hours back. Could you believe that child would set an alarm and call me three hours later to wake me up for class? I would lie and say I was moving just to get him off the phone. Turnover and go back to sleep until the afternoon. He tried to be a good boyfriend. The days I shared that I had not made it to class, he would "punish" me by refusing to talk to me until the next day.

That was his way of encouraging me to get to class. I did not have time for him or his tactics. He was the reason I could not wake up on time. On top of that, he was not even on campus, so he was just asking for me to lie. Did you make it to class? Sure. How was class? Great. What did you learn? Everything. See how simple that was. He was not on campus so he would not know any different. That is until I was on the phone with him walking through campus and came across a classmate who greeted me by saying, "Damn Joness, we aint seen you in class in a month or so". I was stuck. Evan was in my ear saying, "I heard that shit. Talk to your friends and call me back with your explanation". I was over it. But by then I had mastered crying on cue, so I just shed a few tears and made him realize how it was not my fault but his. That semester he honestly thought he was my daddy. He got upset because I would not "ask" him if I could go places. "Sir, you Ain't my daddy and I didn't even call and ask him". I felt like I was being courteous for informing him of my decisions and where I would be but asking did not sit well with me. By October I had secured my ride with an upper-classman to Tallahassee for FAMUs homecoming. An event I was not willing to miss. I had plans on linking with my family and staying lit. The original plans were for us to leave Daytona that Thursday evening. That way, we would only miss one day of class. Didn't matter to me. I was barely making class when I was right there on campus. On Wednesday afternoon she called me and informed me the plans had changed and if I wanted to ride with her, I had one hour before the departure. "Cool, I'm packing now". Called my daddy and let him know I was about to hit the road. He said, "aight do your thang and be safe". Evan on the other hand had to give me the third degree about how he did not feel that was the best decision for me. "That's not even your school so why do you have to go to their homecoming"? "You're going to be missing too many classes. I think you should just stay there". He was not from Florida, so he did not understand that FAMUs homecoming was one event you do not miss. Plus, he was convinced it had to be a boy at that school I was trying to get to. It was true, I had a slida up there but that was not the point. I was going to spend time with my big brother and our cousins, and I did not need his permission. The last thing he said as I finished packing, "If you go, don't call me until you make it back to Daytona Beach". "Aight cool. Love you". I ran downstairs and hopped in the car. We made it to Tallahassee in record time. I called my brother and he picked me up at the Tallahassee mall. That weekend we partied and danced, and I went and played spades with my lil friend. That Friday afternoon Evan called me in a fit. "Why haven't I heard from you"? I was so confused. I was still in Tallahassee, so I was just following his rules. "You told me not to call you, so I didn't". He was so mad. "You know that's not what I meant. And what is all that noise? It's that middle of the day". It was homecoming and set Friday, so you know the music was swangin '. I told him, "From now on I need you to say what you mean and mean what you say." I ended the conversation swiftly so I could get back to the party. He was not about to ruin my good time. That night I went to spend more time with lil friend. It got late and he asked me if I wanted to just stay. He stayed in the same complex as my brother, so I just walked back over there to get my "spend the night bag". It was a little after 1am and I woke Gerry to inform him I would be back in the morning. My brother sat up and said, "Get yo ass in this bed". I was shocked. In all my eighteen years he had never pulled the big brother card on me. We were always equal and just enjoyed life as it came. Nevertheless, I complied. I walked back to my lil slida's house to gather all my things. I was clowned because I had to comply with my brother's instructions. That was cool. I knew my brother loved me and had my best interest at heart so who was I to buck the system? Besides, I was a virgin. I had never spent the night with a man in my life and I was playing a dangerous game. I knew I was not ready to lose my virginity. Even if I was, especially not with him. I just enjoyed his conversation and the attention he gave. It helped me pass time and perfect my flirt. That did not mean I needed to lay with him. I was cool to cuddle and allow him to hold me, that was a privilege in itself. Outside of that, anything sexual was a no go. As an adult I now understand if I would have stayed with him that would have been sending the wrong signals. Thank

God my brother was there to help make a better decision for me. I chuckled all the way back to Gerry's house. "He really just pulled the big brother card on me". I guess I was not as grown as I thought. That weekend ended and I made it back to campus just in time to miss class again. I talked to Evan all the way back home. He was simply happy I made it back in one piece.

The highlight of each week was walking to the mail room to pick up my routine letter from Donovan. I had never written so many handwritten letters in my life, but this is what I honestly looked forward to. The group of friends I had attained was honestly sick of hearing his name. "It's always Donovan this, and Donovan that, and Donovan about to graduate". They would pick at me as if I were wrong for missing my better half. He was not there with me, so they did not understand our relationship. It is true though; I did talk about him every chance I would get. But It was nice to acquire more friends. The athletes in our group naturally gravitated towards me. The band members held a special place in my heart. Daddy was a drum major at Albany State University, played the saxophone and graduated from Bethune Cookman so they were overly loved by me. Out of all the students I ran across no one could have ever told me it would be a girl that vibed with me the most. I was never the girl to have too many girlfriends. But Destiny Stevens seemed to be my twin flame. We had the same interest, embodied the same sarcasm, and understood the same cynical humor. She instantly became my dawg. We were partners at Bethune Cookman. Whatever one had, we shared, never let each other go without and pulled each other through classes. Although if I'm being honest, she was doing most of the pulling. Our attachment was as if I had grown another limb. We were always together; she instantly became family and would even walk to my dorm to drag me out of bed at seven in the morning. After we established this relationship, it was not too long after that we began traveling. Neither of us had a vehicle and we were too young to rent cars. So, I would reserve them and have one of my older cousins rent it in their names. It was not like we were attending big events or had major plans. We were just bored college students stuck in Daytona

Beach. So, we would travel to get a change of scenery. Every Thursday we would hit the road to a different city. Orlando, Jacksonville, Atlanta. Anywhere but campus. We would spend the weekend living our best lives. Drag back into the city late Sunday night and be too tired to make it out of bed Monday morning. If you are paying attention to the schedule, I'm sure you're doing the math right. I had class every day and most classes were Monday, Wednesday, and Friday. Due to my extensive and elaborate travel schedule I was only making it to those courses on Wednesday. only If the weather was right and Maury wasn't on. I know, my priorities were all fucked up. But I was living the dream. I was traveling, partying, cramming for exams and in a relationship with a boy who lived on the other side of the country. So naturally I met someone on campus to help entertain me. He was cool and it was not anything major. We just vibed and had a standing date night every week on the same day and time. Every Wednesday Dennard Marks would pull up to Joyner Hall at 6pm to take me to red lobster. It was our weekly fix of seafood. We were both in a relationship and were not looking to be anything more than friends. It was just a weekly dose of being bae. Having the opportunity to get cute and go out. Our grown and sexy moments with our young asses. That is until Evan found out and made my date nights abruptly end. The weekend he we met at orientation he apparently made a few more friends. Dominique and Cat. He had been bragging about our relationship to them and even sent them a few photos of me. So, he had them on campus spying on me. That night after our last date I made it back to my dorm, Evan called my phone and said, ` `That's a nice car you just got out of". I was so confused, "What you mean". He was blunt, "Joness don't play dumb. That sky blue crown Vic sitting on 22s. As a matter of fact, you got on some nice shoes. So where are you coming from"? I was stuck dead in my tracks, "Evan, are you here"? He laughed, "Nah, one of my homies just sent me a picture of my girlfriend and said I might find it interesting". I was so pissed. He had this bitch Cat on campus watching me and reporting my moves. The worst part about it was I had no clue who she was, so I didn't even know who

I needed to be watching for. That night was filled with tear filled explanations, a breakup, and no sleep. He called me early the next morning to apologize to me. He
realized how wrong he was for having them monitor me. He said sorry for hurting my feelings and we were cool. That is typically what the strength of a few tears would get you.

In November of 2008 I was 18 years old and was now old enough to vote. On election day classes were canceled and the school was concerned with getting souls to the polls. That morning we all woke bright and early, tied up our sneakers and had breakfast in the quad. Our president Dr. Trudie Kibbe Reed shared an encouraging word, and we all bowed our heads in a prayer. At 8:30am, as a university, we marched one mile from "The Ave" at Bethune Cookman University to Daytona Beach Regional Library. We stood in line for hours. In true HBCU fashion, it was a party until the sun went down. The DJs were out, music was swangin, free food was offered, and votes were casted. It was 4:00pm before I made it into a booth, but the experience was well worth it. That evening, we all showered up and prepared to watch the results for the election. We sat up on the edge of our seats all night, and a little after midnight with 52.92% of the popular vote, we had just voted in our first black president. I will never forget where I was that night. The Ave was lit. Jezzy blasted from every speaker on campus. "My president is black, my Lambo's blue And I be god damn if my rims Ain't too". There was a full-blown celebration on the quad for about three hours. We had just helped make history. Classes were canceled again the next day, so of course we continued to celebrate.

That winter I made it home for Christmas and had to adjust to being under my parents' roof again. I had to monitor my cussing, readjust my attitude, and get used to being told what to do. My entire focus was on getting back to Daytona Beach. Although I had not checked my grades during the entire break, I knew it was at least one failing grade on there. Because I was not sure how the grades were being dispensed, I spent that entire break on edge. I checked the mail at nanny's house each day. By the end of the break, nothing came. It did not even occur to me to log onto the computer and check virtually. Although all my parents were continually inquiring about the grades, I was okay with the uncertainty. Ignorance is bliss. Christmas day was fun. Daddy and Ms. Celine threw the annual day after Christmas fish fry. Everyone was home from school, so the house was packed. All the children who were still in the house, every aunt and cousin, God brother, ex-athletes, and close friend. Everyone made their way to 34th and Deleuil for a little love and fun. Music was blasting, fish was dropping, and drinks were being poured. We would all reminisce on past track meets as we sat around the card table. This was my first break home from an HBCU and the first time I felt confident enough to run spades with my family. I played decently. Our oldest cousin RoShard still had to learn me a thing or two. Those moments were the definition of the good old days. Not a care in the world or a schedule to keep. A day filled with love and limited drama. One of those days we pray would never cease. But all good things must come to an end.

The first of the year came and I began to pack my bags to return to Daytona Beach. Before my departure I had a date scheduled with Evan. The spring semester arrived quicker than we expected, and he touched down in Tampa, Fl on January 2nd. He was staying with his aunt and her family until it was time to return to campus. After about an hour of asking and convincing, Nanny let me borrow her car to pay him a visit. He was out in Carrollwood, so it took me a minute to reach him. I was anxious and nervous all wrapped up in one. This was the person I experienced so much drama with in such a short amount of time. I was not sure how he was going to respond. As I pulled up, I was greeted by his smiling face. We stood outside and hugged for what seemed like an eternity. He kissed me, which threw me off guard. I had only been kissed once before in my senior year by a high school friend who was in a relationship. This was new territory for me. Throughout that semester

I engaged in conversations and indulged in meaningless flirting with a couple of men. But this level of connection and affection was foreign. It was sensual and intentional and all that I felt I had lacked. As much as I wanted his touch, I felt my body close like a clam. He hugged me, kissed me on the cheek as he walked me inside to introduce me to his family. They were a little different but a lot of fun. We sat in their living room for about an hour and got acquainted before Evan requested Steak n' Shake. Apparently, they did not have them in LA, and it was now his favorite place to eat. We sat in that restaurant in total bliss. We planned our lives for the upcoming semester and compared our schedules. He had been recruited on the football team, so he was going to be busy. We had twenty-four hours before we were on campus together and made plans to get a room that weekend at the beach. Some extended time alone was just what we needed.

The next morning, we packed the car and hopped on I-4 heading East. Once again, I was accompanied by my mother and auntie Arianna. Upon our arrival we were instructed to head to student accounts. Apparently, I did not have enough financial aid funds remaining for spring tuition. They explained how they transferred money from my financial aid package in the fall for tuition, room, and board. For me to stay I would have to come out of pocket about 13k. This was with every grant and loan under the sun. we called nanny and she explained I had right at that amount remaining in my savings. If I chose to use it to pay tuition, I would be a true broke college student. Or I could keep the funds in my account and return home and attend Hillsborough Community College. Fuck That! I had a taste of freedom and fun and I was not about to run home and give all of that up. We drove straight to the bank. "May I have a cashier's check please". All the adults instructed me to take my time and reconsider. "Ma'am, can you make that out to Bethune Cookman University". I did not have time to play with them. I will not change my mind or run home tucking my tail. I want to be great. That will not happen if I return home to stay. Once we arrived back on campus to make that payment with only $170 remaining in my checking, I was relieved, for all of three seconds. While auntie and I were making the payment, Orjury ass disappeared and went and got answers to her questions. She met a man on campus and asked how she could get access to my grades because they never came over the break. He escorted her to student affairs and printed them out there. Just like that I found out that I was on academic probation. That first semester filled with traveling, partying, dating and some great sleep, proved to be horrible academically. I was hurt, disappointed in myself and extremely embarrassed. But it was far from a surprise. That first semester I walked into the library to study maybe ten times. I was enrolled and had fun, but I was not a real student. Orjury viewed my grades, laughed, and said, "Oh this is why they never came". She picked up the phone to share the grades with my daddy and his only warning was, "Fuck up again and you coming home". The first semester of my college career I earned two F's, two D's and one C. surprisingly, no one was pissed. I spent the entire break fearing their response and they barely flinched. I guess That was the difference I had to understand. This was a new ballgame. The grades I earned were for me, not them. The village got me through high school. They did their parts. What I accomplished from that point going forward would be entirely up to me. On that day, at that moment, I refocused. I vowed to myself that going forward I would at least try. It is one thing to struggle through a class because it is not your subject. Even if it's not, I would still have to put my best foot forward. I had not honestly tried or worked hard at shit. I knew I was smarter than that display, it was just piss poor effort. It was time to change.

Following our quick embrace and chipper goodbyes, I sprinted across campus to meet Evan in Bronson hall, the athletic dorm. That afternoon we were picked up and taken to Seabreeze apartments, the hangout spot. That December, right before we departed school, Destiny, her boyfriend Barron, and our friend Don all got an apartment. They shared a two-bedroom, one bathroom which was utopia at school. That space allowed us to be as grown as we thought we were. We were all still eighteen but, in those moments, we were the adults. Destiny and Barron had recently broken up and were both still on the lease. That fact made the house slightly uncomfortable at times, but we survived. Hell, they were in that limbo area still. Although I advised they refrained from moving together they went against my better judgement which made for some rather interesting days ahead. Once we made it to the apartment, I introduced Evan to everyone. "Dan, Destiny, Barron, Sidney, this is my boyfriend Evan".

We stayed there that night and quickly got readjusted to college life. Grabbed a bottle and a deck of cards. We ordered some food and stayed up all night. It was Friday, I could start off on the right foot come Monday morning.

The following afternoon Don and Destiny dropped us off at the beach. We got a room and spent the day laying in each other's arms. We had hard conversations about that crown Vic again and why my relationship was new news to my friends. He did not understand how I spent all my time with these people and none of them knew I had a man. "You've been out here living single and that's over now, I'm here". I thought that shit was so cute. He was really trying to tell me what to do. He asked me a few times if there was anything important, I needed to tell him so he would not have to later find out. Nothing of grave importance came to mind, so we kissed and agreed this is what it was going to be. We chose us, just him and me. I went into that weekend sure that I was going to lose my virginity. But I was not ready, and I was glad he understood. We stayed in that room locked away for two days. Everything was great, until it was not.

The next five weeks flew by in a blur. I was retaking courses, so I had been left by my cohort. I was a slightly better student. I still preferred to stay home but every time I wanted to miss class Destiny reminded me that I paid for those courses out of pocket. She was right so I got my ass up and hiked the one mile from the apartment to the university. Can't be great if you don't at least try. We had class, Evan had practice and every evening we found a reason to celebrate. By then, Don and Barron had begun selling weed. We were actually living in the trap house. It took us a few weeks to catch on. Of course, I did not live there, but I lived there. I was still assigned to the dorm but of course I was never there. I was trying to hold up my end of the bargain by checking in with Camille, but every time I stopped by her room she was never there. So, I went on about my business. Evan and I were still arguing. He didn't appreciate my nonchalant responses to his attempts at drawing some emotions, so we continued to butt heads. The first big clash was about three weeks in, and it was completely unnecessary. We completed a successful week in my opinion. I made it to each class, turned in homework on time and spent free time with friends. It was Friday evening, and I was waiting for Evan to get out of practice. We made plans to meet at the apartment and have a movie night. It was 7pm by the time he arrived. He walked in the door fully dressed and out of breath. He looked at me and explained that he was leaving to take Cat on a date. "Excuse me"? I was so confused. If you are taking the next bitch on a date, why would you come here? He explained that he was taking her to Cold Stone and would come back once they were done. "Okay, bring me back some cookies n cream". He was not about to get a rise out of me. He was so determined to get an argument and rise in emotions. I did not love like that and to me it made no sense. He felt if I didn't fight and argue with him it wasn't real. I had enough drama in my childhood for a lifetime. I did not need this excessiveness in my life. He stood there looking dumb and eventually walked out the front door. As soon as he left, I called my brother to complain. "Brother you wouldn't believe what this dumbass just showed up and said". Of course, I was pissed but I wasn't going to let him win. He was trying to make me upset so I refused to give him that satisfaction. I'll call and cry to my brother so when he returns, I can maintain my composure. He was back and knocking on the door thirty minutes later. To this day I am still not sure if he was with Cat. all I know is he came back with my ice cream and he was upset. "I can't believe you let me just leave. I told you I was going out with the next bitch and you could not care less. You don't give a fuck about me". He had some nerves. "You can't believe I let you leave, and I can't believe you left. Now we are two people who can't believe each other, so what's next". We sat on the sofa and proceeded with our movie night. He held me as I enjoyed my cookies and cream. We decided to be good until the next episode.

On top of class, relationships, and our mandatory dedicated time to spades, we were also required to complete community service hours. Bethune Cookman University required each freshman to volunteer in the community. I figured it made sense since it was the same community we were there terrorizing with our horrible decisions. Destiny and I decided to volunteer at adult academy, a high school a half a mile from the college campus. The school was designed for pregnant teens and teen mothers. While enrolled, the girls completed standardized work to receive their high school diploma. They were also enrolled in caregiver courses to help strengthen their mothering skills. We appreciated the set up and offered our time tutoring a few girls who were struggling with their classwork. This time was always a nice escape from our own drama. It also served as a weekly reminder to make the best of our time in Daytona. We were not too much older than those girls. At the rate we were going, we were only one bad decision, drunken night or make up after a fight away from being in their position ourselves. That spring we spent eighty hours of our time at the adult academy. We were broke college students, in a small town and moving fast. We needed those humbling moments.

That February we were back to our antics. We were itching to get out of that city. So, we booked a car that my cousin Royce rented, and we headed to Atlanta for a girl's weekend. I do not know how I made friends with all these children who could not drive. Since they were from Atlanta, they rode the MARTA everywhere and never received their license. Cool with me. I love to drive so I was down for the long ride. There was only one issue in our plans. Daddy called me the day we were planning to leave and said,

"Don't take your ass outside of Daytona Beach. You did enough travel last semester, now stay still and study". I felt awful. I never went directly against one of my daddy's commands. But we already had the rental car and made plans. "Okay y'all, after we come back from Atlanta, we can't go anywhere else". This time in a change of events, we attended our Friday morning classes before we hit the road. We left entirely too late, and they fell asleep as soon as we got on the road. I was pissed. Not only were they not helping me drive, but they also were not even helping me stay awake. It was 10:30 at night when I ran past a sign that said 100 miles to Atlanta. "Damn, Still"? I was tired, they were snoring, so I began to hit it. Before I knew it, I was running 105 up I-75. not too long after, I flew past the police. They came and got me immediately. My heart was racing so fast, and I almost pissed on myself. "Young lady is there a reason why you are going this fast"? He had me step out of the car to complete a sobriety test. "Sir, I'm not drunk, I'm just trying to get my friends home and they can't drive". I played like I wasn't aware how fast I was going. "Young lady you can still smell the rubber burning. And where is Royce". "In Daytona Beach". He rented us the vehicle, but I was underage, so we didn't add my name as a driver. He chastised me and I turned on the waterworks, he wrote me a ticket and told me to slow down. I got back into the vehicle and immediately called my big brother. I was scared and did not know what to do. "Joness you just got your refund. Go to Atlanta and have some fun. When you get back home pay it on Monday". Cool. If Gerry was good, I was always fine. Like an idiot, I threw the ticket into the glove compartment as if the car were mine. Hopped back on the road and made it to Atlanta in no time. We got there in the middle of the night. We stayed with Destiny's brother and his family. Fell asleep around 5 and we were up by 7. Got up and ran around the city all day. Stopped to visit her family and some of mine. Later that night we picked up one of her old flings and caught a movie. We were sitting in front of his house at 1 in the morning when my daddy called me frantically and said, "Misty just got shot".

I was stuck in disbelief. We had had our moments and never really learned how to be sisters, but I didn't want anything bad to happen to her. "See this is why yall are supposed to be where you say you are going to be. We gave her ass permission to go to Brandon for a teen party, and she was in Nuccio at the park in a shootout. We are heading to the hospital right now to see how bad it is". Of course, I felt like shit. He's on the phone saying we should be where we say we are going to be, and I was in a completely different state. I immediately went and grabbed our bags, got some gas and a pack of 5-hour energy drinks. I took one, said a prayer and hit the road. It was now 2:30 in the morning and I was operating off two hours of sleep. But I had to make it back to Daytona beach. On the way home I was speeding, fell asleep wishing they would stay up and keep me company. I saw the sun rise as I entered Volusia county. Still no update about her state. Not a single person would answer their phone. My nerves would not let me rest so Destiny and I got back in the car and hopped on I-4. I pulled into Tampa an hour and 45 minutes later on a Sunday all for them to call and say she got shot in the ass. The ass. She had enough of that to lose. I was glad she was okay and thanked god for that comedic relief.

On a positive note, Donovan had just made it back into town, so I flipped the car and rushed towards my bestest friend. As we pulled up, I drove towards this beautiful black grown man. He was not the little boy who left for bootcamp. I am talking about, he looked good. Destiny was up in arm that I let her meet him while she was looking a mess. I was upset. I was in a relationship and he was my bestest, but I needed her to stop looking at him. He was mine and I was not happy to share. When he embraced me, it felt like home. Like since he had been gone, I'd been holding my breath. We hung out all evening and I got about two hours of rest. At 7pm we had to turn around and head back to school so I could make curfew. After that long ass eventful weekend, I was just trying to make it back to my bed. We made it back just in time. Returned the car, ticket, and all, made it back to my dorm and immediately began to snore.

A week or so later our entire little family at Bethune Cookman began to go up in flames. One evening we were all at the house relaxing. The boys were upfront playing call of duty, Destiny was in her room watching a movie, and I was stretched across the bed in the back room watching 8 Mile. towards the middle of the movie our friend John came into the room with me so he could talk to one of his "friends". He laid across the bed with me as he giggled and smiled uncontrollably. I was happy to see him happy. In our friends group we had all begun relationships with one another, so John was always the seventh wheel. It was nice to see someone entertain him for once. During that conversation, he began speaking loudly and I asked him to lower his voice so I could continue to enjoy the movie. He sat up, snatched the remote and muted the volume. We began to wrestle over the remote and messed up the covers on the bed. Just then, Evan walked in with a look of disgust. He turned around and went back to the front of the house. I immediately thought, "Here we go with this shit". I know how it looked, I'm not dumb. I was on the bed, playing wrestling with another man while my boyfriend was in the front of the house. when He walked in, we looked guilty as shit. However, I am not that rude and disrespectful and don't nobody want John's ass. That's why he was the one in our group single. I snatched the remote and continued to watch my movie. A few moments later Evan yelled, "Joness, come watch me play". I walked upfront grudgingly. I Sat next to him and tried to be sweet. "Bae, I'm watching the movie and it's almost to the best part, I'll come back out here once it goes off". Everyone knows you watch 8 Mile for the final battle. I did not watch that entire movie to not see B. Rabbit win in the end. Evan King was not trying to hear that. "I want you to watch me play this game. Just sit and cheer for me". I complied for about five minutes. Who in the hell wants to sit and watch Call of Duty? Not me! I got up and went back to see the end of the movie. He was fuming. Naomi, you really about to go back to the room with that nigga? I knew it was nothing and on top of that Evan was not my daddy. I do what the fuck I want to do. As his girlfriend I tried to appease him and take his feelings into account, but that was about it. He Ain't run shit. I sat on the edge of the bed to watch the last ten minutes or so. Evan sat up front being hyped up by Barron. "If that were my girl it wouldn't have gone down like that. My dude, you just gonna accept that level of disrespect"? Once the movie was over, I returned to watch them play that dumbass game. According to him, that was me admitting my level of guilt. He was fuming. I thought that shit was cute but unnecessary. Again, didn't nobody want John's ass. We sat up and argued all night. After a couple hours of disagreeing and a few good tears, we finally laid down to sleep. We ended the night in routine, with his arms wrapped tightly around me.

Following that evening the tides began the shift. The boys began to exclude John from our nightly events and Evan was distant. I could not believe he was being so childish. I thought we had gotten over it. He had the boys coming up to chastise me. "Sis I can't believe you would try bro like that. You know he is still mad. He's waiting on a full explanation of what actually went down". I wasn't trying to hear that. I had already said my peace, he just had to be mad on his own.

Around that time the boys started selling weed out of the house. Destiny and I were in the dark for about a week before we figured it out. They were attempting to "protect" us by not giving us details. We did not like it and it's not like there was anything we could do to make them stop but we didn't want to be left in the dark. We at least needed to know what was going on. We were in college and it was just weed. It was everywhere, everyone smoked it. Although I hated that stench, I had even gotten used to it. However, I personally did not smoke. I tried it one time on my 19th birthday. Everyone else was inebriated and we had no access to any alcohol. My cousins would not answer the phone and I was over being the only sober one. Hell, after all It was MY birthday. I tried it. I had to have hit it three or four times. It was disgusting and on top of that, I felt nothing. Apparently, I didn't inhale, and the entire house was up trying to coach me through. They wanted me to try again and again. I declined. That wasn't my drug of choice. I know we all have our vices and at that point, alcohol was mine. I knew how to drink. I was not gonna spend time trying to learn how to smoke. After all, I had gotten too accustomed to referring to all my druggy friends' crackheads. I was not about to join in.

I was drinking, they were selling and smoking. Apparently, the law was not something we were too concerned with. Not too long after, it caught up with us all. Late one evening the boys left the house on a mission. While we were sleeping, they decided to go be reckless. Once they returned to the house, Evan laid behind me with his heart racing. I woke up immediately, "What's wrong with you"? He refused to share and promised to tell me in a month or two. I was terrified. Whatever it was, I knew if he could not tell me, it was not good. Within 48 hours they all ended up in handcuffs. I was forced to call his family in California to inform them their son was locked up. At that time, I had matured academically. I was honestly doing well in class. But now here I was heading to the prison attending something called a first appearance. I knew as soon as my daddy got wind of this, he would have my head. I had to bail a nigga out of jail. Are you serious? I left Tampa to get away from that crazy environment and I was still stuck in the middle of some shit. The crazy thing is women typically lose their mind for the man they are sleeping with, but I was still a virgin. I was not even getting the dick. I was just a foolish child who thought she was in love. We spent a day and a half trying to figure out how to get him. Once he was out, we had about twelve hours of peace.

Once we returned to campus the next morning, we were informed he had been expelled from school. The administration and coaching staff were informed of his arrest and he was to be off campus by sundown. His uncle showed up within a few hours to take him back to Tampa. He had to stay within the state because he still had an open case. That day all I wanted to do was be a regular college student. Attend class, do some work, walk through the library. You know, normal shit. Unfortunately, that day I had to help my boy-friend pack so he could leave me.

We had already done the long-distance thing. We knew how to keep each other entertained on the phone. Although he was not as far this time, he was still not on campus with me. Not too long after his departure did Destiny and I start entertaining Ray and Quan. they were also freshmen on campus and had become regular customers for Barron and don. One weekend, the boys went to Atlanta and failed to inform their customers. Ray and Quan came by looking to cop an ounce and found us alone in the apartment. They came in as they complained and made themselves comfortable. We found a movie and stayed up clowning all night. They stayed with us that night and the next. We were just enjoying being in mixed company. Once the boys returned home, we continued our visits. This time they would come in the evening while they were working at the beachside burger King. Evan was out of town, but Don and Barron were left in charge of "watching me". Ray and I were just friends, but I knew we were too close for comfort.

Looks like the shit hit the fan all in one week. I was staying every night at the apartment and had not caught up with Camille the entire semester. Like I said, I was trying to keep up my end of our bargain, but she was never around for me to check in with her. In March, our dorm mother, Ms. Gladys took it upon herself to call Nanny at 2:30AM to inform her that I had missed curfew 47 nights in a row. Forty-seven nights. Of course, nanny went ballistic and attempted to contact me but of all the inopportune times in the world, my phone was dead. She called my daddy, and they began calling around Tampa, waking up the city trying to find my whereabouts. I was sound asleep in the apartment with my friends. In hindsight, it baffles me why they were all panicking. They might not have known my exact location, but they knew I was alive and well. At that time in my life, I talked with each of them at least an hour a day. That explains why I never had enough time for a proper studying regime. Anyway, Auntie Arianna put her investigative skills to use and found Destiny's phone number. They finally called her phone and got into contact with me at 5:45AM. Nanny expressed her disappointment in my decisions and demanded I go straight to the dorm once I woke up. I could not believe the dorm mother. Why would she wait so long before saying something and why would she call in the middle of the night? I know I was the one in the wrong, but I felt it could have been handled in a more productive manner. There was no reason to call and scare my grandmother out of her sleep. I know she had my personal phone number on file. What I found out later that day was the fact that Camille graduated in the fall and had not returned in the spring. They had not found a replacement for her so Ms. Gladys had been conducting her check ins since then. To be honest, I know I missed a lot more than 47 nights, but I wasn't about to correct that fact. Sitting in her office the next morning, she lectured me on the importance of being responsible and accountable. Informed me that my family would not appreciate my actions and I needed to begin to conduct myself like a young adult. Mind you, that is what I was trying to do by minding my business until she stuck her nose in it. She went on to say, "Ms. Pratt, if you remember there is a 50-dollar fee associated with every missed night of curfews". She asked me if my disappearing acts were a cry for help. "No ma'am, I'm good. Just don't really like being in here". She continued by saying, "Well if this were a cry for help, we could consider waiving the fees. if not, they will be added to your student accounts and need to be settled prior to next semester". Just doing some quick math I realized I owed the school over two bands just because I did not want to sleep in that dorm. "It's a cry for help! I've been lost since I got here". She waived the fees and made me move my room to the first floor next to her office so she could keep an eye on me. It worked for all of three nights. I did not want to stay in the dorm with the girls I had gotten to know and love in the fall semester. I damn sure didn't want to stay in this new room with these females who were upset I was impeding upon their extra space. So back to the apartment I went, for about one week.

That next week was doomsday. I had already been cursed by all my parents and clowned with my brother about them tripping. My grades were still intact, so I did not know what else they wanted from me. I was in college which meant I should be allowed to be as grown as I wanted to be. apparently, they had not received that memo. But this week they were not the problem, we were running from Barron. He had gotten word that we were entertaining Quan and Ray and was not a happy camper. He texted the four of us and promised to kill us by the end of the day. Let's just say, we knew he had an ample amount of means to do so. That was my last day in their apartment. I went one last time to collect all my belongings and head back to the dorm where I was supposed to be. If you remember, he and Destiny were broken up, but he was upset because we "clowned" him with one of his homeboys. I was guilty because I knew and wrong because I had a boyfriend. Of course, he was the first person to call Evan. Evan played it cool. He was only concerned about my health and wellbeing. That is up until the charges against him were dropped. His case was still open, and I was his alibi. He needed me for his freedom. As soon as the charges were dropped two weeks later, he dropped me. I do not blame him. I deserved it. We had no business being a relationship anyway. I was enjoying my freedom and was determined to keep it.

I ended that semester with 2 As, 2 Bs and 1 C. In all the chaos I managed to rehab my GPA just enough to maintain my freedom the upcoming school year. At the end of the semester, I packed my things and headed back to Tampa bay, home of the drama, my childhood trauma and dysfunction which was apparently embedded in my DNA.

Once I made it home, I stopped by Nanny's house first. Making it home and not being ashamed of my grades came with a new level of pride and satisfaction. True, I'd been through the shits that semester but at least it didn't end in an academic suspension. In a change of events my mother was there to greet me. We laughed and talked about my first-year college experience. I always enjoy her in those moments. If nothing else, she knows how to have fun.

More importantly, she got me. Somehow, she knew that in those last month's I had lost my virginity. According to her, I proved it in my attitude and demeanor. I did not see a difference. I slept with Evan during my last visit with him before he returned to L.A. just foolish. That was the last time I ever laid eyes on him, so it was the wrong decision to make, but that was my first boyfriend and that's a memory we share.

Orjury invited me out onto Nanny's side porch to continue our chat. She pulled out an envelope as she lit a cigarette and asked, "So how was your trip to Georgia"? I damn near choked on spit. "My what"? She laughed and pulled out a copy of my ticket. After that crazy weekend and all the following events, I forgot all about that damn ticket. She proceeded to read it and asked me where I was headed to in such a hurry to catch a 1700-dollar ticket. "$1700 Dollars"? Are they crazy? I was scared as shit. That refund check was long gone, and I did not have a job. I had no clue as to how it would be paid. "Well according to this letter, you owe a 100-dollar late fee, and it is due in two weeks or they will suspend your license". I was so over her. First, I do not know who gave her permission to open my damn mail. Second, if you are going to break the law and read someone else's mail, at least do it with good intent. She held onto that letter until I got home to say something. Now I do not have that much cash. "Didn't your daddy tell you not to leave Daytona Beach"? Oh, so this was my punishment. That makes sense.

We ended the conversation, and I immediately called my brothers to explain the dilemma. Christian offered to pay for my ticket so I could keep my license. Once daddy found out he intervened and would not let Christian help me. According to all the grown folks, if he would have paid the ticket for me, I would never understand the value in having a valid license. Two weeks flew by and I was now holding a suspended license. I could not believe they just let that happen. Not only did they not help me, but they also blocked my help and taunted me about my lack of mobility the entire summer. I was a 19-year-old home from college for the summer without transportation. You could only imagine how miserable I was.

Life lessons always come with a steep price and that summer; I got the message. Listen to what I am told, slow down on the road and if nothing else change my permanent address on my license.

It was the middle of the summer before we were back to regularly scheduled programming with my mother's drama. Although I experienced my own self-inflicted problems and pain while in school, this was always a little more significant and consequential. I had been staying at my daddy's house the entire summer, so I made a point to go over and spend some time with my grandmother. Nanny had become one of my closest friends since I was away at school. She even learned how to text more rapidly so we would talk all day. That night I stayed with her so we could enjoy each other's company. Once it got late, she went to bed, and I stayed up in the front room. Uncle Jr. was in his room in bed too. A little after midnight my mother stormed into the house higher than I had ever personally witnessed. She was extremely happy at first. She told me to go to the back room so she could sleep in peace and watch Law and Order SVU. cool with me. I did not want to be in her presence in that state anyway. Once I got to the back room, I quickly realized I was in there without a television. There were only three cable boxes in the house. The living room, Uncle Jr.'s room and nanny's room. So, I got comfortable on the bed and continued to scroll through my phone for entertainment. A few moments later my mother stubbled through the room door and asked why I was not watching tv. "The box is in Uncle Jr.'s room but I'm fine I have my phone". She proceeded to move through the house in a whirlwind. In one movement She burst into his room. "Jr. wake your ass up and put the box in the back room so Naomi can watch tv". He woke up and did so grudgingly. "Uncle, I was fine, I don't know why she came in there to bother you. I'm sorry". He replied, "it's fine baby. See you in the morning" as he continued to sleepwalk to his room. Once I turned on the tv I realized one of the cords must have been displaced because it still was not working, but I wasn't pressed. Ten minutes later Orjury came to the back room again and caught wind. You would think someone in her state would want to sit down and just enjoy the ride. But not my mother. She was determined to disturb everyone's peace. "Jr.! didn't I tell you to fix this damn tv" as she swung open his door and turned the light on. "Orjury, I'm asleep, damn". "I'm honestly fine, mama you can leave him alone". He pushed her out of his room and locked the door. She got progressively louder calling him all kinds and bitches and hoes as she kicked a hole in his door. I begged them to lower their voices. Nanny was the only one in that house who had to get up and go to work later that morning. By this time, it was after 1 AM and her alarm would ring at 4:00am. "will you all please let my grandmother sleep". By that time, it was too late. Nanny emerged from her bedroom door concerned and confused. "Orjury, calm down. What's wrong"? By this time Uncle Jr. was furious. "Mama you better get her, or I swear I'm going to kill her. I'm sick of her shit". My mother was behind nanny taunting uncle Jr. and daring him to hit her. Nanny ran into her room and grabbed her purse. She pulled uncle jr. out of the house and transported him to auntie Arianna's. One would like to think at that moment she was saving her son. Saving him from any charges he would catch from beating Orjury's ass. That was not the case, at least not in my eyes. She was saving her daughter, once again. Orjury was the one who came into the house and disturbed our peace. She was the one who honestly needed her ass beat. Nanny should have let him hit her. But no. She removed him from the environment to let her daughter be. And in doing so she left me, in the house, with the high lady. They were gone and off to their safety and comfort and I was stuck in the house with the remnants of my mother in the form of a full-blown crackhead. She knew how to clear a room. Then play victim when no one wants to deal with her. I sat back on the bed in disbelief. I could not believe they just left me. Once again, she came bursting into the room. "Stay your ass back here. As a matter of fact, give me your phone". Apparently, she forgot I was grown. She said give her my phone like she paid my damn bill. I mean I did not either, auntie Arianna did since the seventh grade. Still, that was not the point. She needed to go sit her high ass down because she did not run shit. I looked at her and chuckled as I said, "nah". By then she was irate. She walked through the house spewing all kinds of threats. I finally got up and put on my shoes. I had been calling around to my siblings for the past hour. None of them would pick up the phone. So, I decided to just walk to daddy's house. It was only a 10–15-minute walk around the block. It was in the middle of the night, but I wasn't scared.

The only demon I had to fear was already there. She followed me through the house and cursed me. She Told me I was weak and advised me not to try her. Demanded me to sit down and dared me to walk out the house. As I walked into the sunroom to gather my things, she shared a few things off her heart. "That's not even your daddy, he's Taylors. He does not love you; he feels sorry for you. You run around that corner like you are a part of their family. Him and that black ass bitch. If you needed blood today, they would not be able to do shit. I am the one who gave you life. And I shouldn't have did that with your stuck up, ungrateful ass. I was supposed to have an abortion. The only reason I had you was because the doctor said I would have a miscarriage. But no, now I'm stuck here with you". I continued to chuckle as I grabbed my bag, "You about twenty years too late". Her words hurt and they cut deep. Once again, she was trying to break me. Thank God I am not that delicate. They say a drunk man will not tell any tales. I just figured the same rules would apply when you're high. Either way, I made it to the front door ready to take my hike. Once I got to the bottom of Nanny's slanted driveway, she grabbed the bottom of my hair and yanked me to the ground. It was the middle of the night and I was in the road fighting with my mother. Our neighbor, Ms. T. came out and grabbed me. She pulled me into her house and said she heard me scream. I just needed that lady to stay away from me. My siblings finally returned my calls and flew around the corner to rescue me. I woke up at daddy's house the next morning scratched up and bruised. Nanny called me and said, "Did you call your mother and apologized yet"? Now Ain't that bout a bitch.

Once sophomore year began, Destiny and I moved into a two-bedroom apartment. We were in the same complex as their apartment our freshman year but in a different building. Against all advice and forewarnings, we became roommates. All the older folks advised against this. They said they did not want us to hinder our friendship. We were now young adults and of course we knew it all. We signed a lease and now had our own set of keys. Nanny and my mother made a few trips to Daytona helping us furnish the apartment with essentials. We had a tv, futon, dining room table and a blowup mattress. Just her and I, and campus was one mile away. We still did not have a vehicle, but hell at that point neither one of us had a license. We walked wherever we needed to go and caught a ride whenever the timing was right. Not long after settling in we met two boys on the other side of the complex. Ray and Ron. Although we were single, these relationships were not like that. It was nice to have some homeboys. They quickly became our rivals in spades, ride to school and sitting partners when we had nothing to do. They both had girlfriends who couldn't stand our presence. They never believed that we were just cool. The boys tried to plan a game night so we could all get acquainted. They came, stayed in the rooms, and eventually summons the boys to the back too. That year, they were our running joke. They eventually made a demand for Ray and Ron to stop visiting us and stay home. The girls did not live there so it is not like they could really run shit. We were still young and immature, so it was funny to us. Even after an ultimatum they wouldn't stay away. They just began to duck and dodge and ignore calls. The girls even did a drive by after midnight. They would come sit and call from the parking lot to make sure they were home. I thought it was so pitiful. But back then I just did not understand. I had been in that one dramatic ass relationship and I thought I loved him, but I never went to that extreme. It was too much like desperate for me.

It was my third semester as a biology major. I was doing better in class and attended more often. The more I attended, the more I realized I did not like it. There was nothing about my courses that piqued my interest. I was kind of just there and going through the motions. Spent most of my free time at the hair salon right off campus. I had grown close to Ms. Tina sitting in her chair fresh-man year and her salon was my hangout spot. I would sit there in my comfort, for good company and advice. Hang out until the sun would go down, get up the next day and repeat. I was still trying it. I Had not yet learned how to be a student. I was even skipping the course taught by my academic advisor. Then I would have the nerve to sit in her office and say I was trying my best. "Ms. Pratt, I haven't seen you actually try yet". She was right. Academically, I did not know how to fight. I did decently in her course the first few weeks. I understood that content and it was easy. As soon as we delved into tougher topics which required me to think it felt like I would shrink. Once I got older, I realized I was suffering from imposter syndrome. Of my siblings and even amongst my friends I seemed to be the one who struggled the most when it came to the books. I had common sense and felt like I knew how to get through life, but class was different. It had been a minute since I felt smart, and my grades proved that I was just average. The truth is, I just did not know what I was doing. I did not even know how to study and had not even tried to manage my time. The days were just passing by. Whatever I did is what got accomplished. I was surviv-ing courses by doing the bare minimum. I didn't read, didn't try, didn't study. I showed up, grasped the information I could. Took exams and gambled my life and future on that. It is evident by all the Cs on my transcript.

I was single that year, but I did talk to a few people. It was Arthur who I called the old man, famous Arron for about a month, and Miami who lived in Atlanta. The old man was 27 and a retired drug dealer. He spent all day fishing on his boat and tended to his family of four once he made it home. That is, after first stopping by to see me. I had had my time in a relationship and determined college was not the time for that. At least not right then. He was not mar-ried, but I knew he had a family. At the age of 19, that aint have shit to do with me. We would talk and text, have a drink whenever he would stop by and bring me a meal. We would even squeeze in a quick game of spades before he had to be on his way. In retrospect,

I knew I was wrong and was not living right. But I had fun. In high school I was damn near a nun, so I was just playing catch up. Famous was the brother of one of Destiny's lil friends. He aint last that long but he left an imprint. He would hold me tight in his arms whenever they would spend the night. I had to be close, and he ensured our legs were entangled throughout the night. He is the reason why till this day I hate sleeping alone. Miami was 29 and had no business entertaining me at 19. He was a truck driver who I spent a few months talking to. I had planned on seeing him during spring break, but my daddy could not believe I wasn't coming home to spend time with him. He even pulled on my heart strings by saying, "I can't believe you're not coming home to be an auntie the one week you're free". So, I had to change my plans. There is not one person who came before Deon.

Going home for spring break allowed me to slow down. Got a chance to catch up with my crazy kin and even spend some well needed time with lifelong friends. I met the twins in elementary school, and we were close even back then. We parted ways in middle school but reunited in 9th grade. Throughout high school we rekindled our friendship and only got closer in college. They live with their parents, two blocks south of us. The grace family. I was an adopted child. Their living room became my sanctuary. In that space with them I had the chance to vent and reminisce. Receive sound advice and whoever wronged me, Chanelle was ready to fight. That person was typically my mother. Like any other visit, this time was no different. By this time, they had added me on the insurance. Medical, dental and vision. This trip home was scheduled to remove all four of my wisdom teeth. Right as I started college, they began to give me hell. So, the dentist decided it was best to remove them all in one visit. My appointment was mid-morning when all the adults were at work. Nanny entrusted my mother with the task of transporting and caring for me. We made it to the appointment on time and the procedure was concluded without a hitch. I rode home without pain, thanks to the laughing gas and laid in Nanny's room to recover and sleep. Orjury left me there to go and pick up my prescription. Nanny gave her a few bucks to pick up my meds, so she said that's what she was going to get. She left me in that house at 12 noon. Swollen mouth, missing teeth, and nothing to eat. In true Orjury fashion she never returned. It was 7:30pm before nanny made it home from work. My mother showed up two days later to check on how I was doing. If it were left up to her, I would have died of starvation and developed an infection. I could have been on my way to a grave and I'm not sure if she would care either way. I mean, she was supposed to abort me.

Once I returned to school, I made the decision to take three classes during the summer. I was attempting to catch up to my cohort. Destiny returned to Atlanta for the summer, so I was stuck in that Podunk town all alone with a broken phone. I was not used to being by myself so that was a lesson all on its own. I was also not okay with missing my family on the track, so I had to make a few things shake. I began to volunteer as a coach with the local AAU track team. That way I was able to fix that itch and secure a ride to the meets on the weekends. That six-week semester flew by fast. Once it ended, I was back home with my unconventional family. By that time big Deon made his way home from prison. He had been arrested a few times for selling to undercovers. Of course, he did not live with us, but he would stop by from time to time to see his son. My child. The one I am convinced was conceived for me. I had not been home for a good two weeks before all hell broke loose. It was four in the morning when my daddy walked into the den to wake me. "go ahead and get up, the police will be here soon". He went on to explain the police were looking for Deon. Apparently, they suspected him of a few cop murders. They had arrived and surrounded the house before I could stretch good. We walked to the front and collected the rest of the house. Daddy walked out in front and instructed us to keep our hands up. Christian carried little Deon out in his arms. We were surrounded by men pointing guns at us. Daddy told them he would not let us walk out until they lowered the guns down. They walked us into the middle of the street to receive our statements. I did not have too much to say.

I personally had not seen him in a little under a decade. We were out there in the cool weather for hours as they tossed our house. Looking for only God knows what. We told them he was not there and wouldn't come. This was not his home. They eventually walked us back in. Naturally, Ms. Celine was sick. There was a city-wide manhunt for her first-born son. Before they left for the first time a detective stood in our doorway and encouraged her to get a message to him to turn himself in. "Ma'am, if we have to track him down, we'll kill him". He was brutal, cold, and honest. It was awful but it was reality. We had visitors coming in and out of the house all day to check on our wellbeing. Everyone who stopped by the house left with a trace. The police even went to my apartment in Daytona and kicked my door in. they sent people to Christian's place in charlotte, grandmas in new Tampa and our auntie in Lakeland. The hunt was on for just under a week. It was big, it was dramatic. It was the same shit we had been doomed to live, just on a grander scale. He eventually turned himself in and they were able to capture him without a kill. My baby was now charged with leading a life as his father's namesake. He was only four and de-served so much more. There was a debate within the family weather or not to change his name. They eventually did nothing and left him with a burden too big for any of us to ever under-stand. He now walks into rooms with individuals and their pre-conceived judgements. He is a black man in America, so that's not anything new. But now, people have additional ammo. Ignorant adults have referred to my baby as the cop killer's son. Just like he was not only four and at home in bed when it occurred. Like he is automatically a menace because of whose kid he is. Like he is pos-sessed by some sort of "bad blood". That same type of "bad blood" that ran through my veins. The same reason the elders never wanted me to drink or smoke or try anything outside of the norm. Because somehow, I was more susceptible to addiction. My mother and father both struggled with their vices, so it only made sense that I would develop the same trend. But they were wrong. I am not them; I am my own person. I was in college, so yes, I drank. I tried it, but no, I don't smoke weed. I have lied, I have cheated, I don't steal. I am not innately bad to my core. I try my hardest to be a good person. I intentionally place myself in others' shoes before passing judgement and try not to hold grudges. Before this thing is over, my baby will also prove the world wrong. Carrying his father's name and all.

When I returned to Daytona beach that fall the tides had shifted. Destiny and I were no longer on the same page. There was tension in our house. I honestly cannot even remember where it started. We had a few disagreements but never full out fights. but We were walking past each other without speaking. Our house was silent unless we had company. I remember we had a few different thoughts on various subjects, she stated she thought I was jealous of her relationship and she did not appreciate me lying about a friend's sexual orientation. She also brought up a conversation I had with my cousin freshman year. She had a big ass, and he asked me did she get off. I told him yeah. At that time, I was young, immature, and naive. I was a virgin and anyone who was not was the definition of getting off to me. I was wrong and I apologized but from that point on our relationship just wasn't right. I made it back to FAMU that fall for homecoming. That trip made up my mind to transfer. I had my time in Daytona and I was thankful for it, but it was time to go and continue to grow. The following Monday I submitted my application. I knew I would get in because I had earned more than sixty credits. I had just received my refund check which I survived off each semester. Destiny and I made money decisions and moved together, but since we were on the outs, I saw no need to include her. I found an apartment in Tallahassee and used those funds to make a deposit instead of paying the rest of Daytona's rent. I received my acceptance letter before thanksgiving and from that point I was just counting down the days. One of my mutual friends tipped her off about my departure which pissed her off. She told me what I was and was not going to do before I could leave. That afternoon Donovan, MY best friend, walked through our front door. Shed called him to vent and he came running. After their first encounter freshman year they tried to be a thing, but it never matured into anything serious. But there he was. In my house, coming to comfort the next female. They left me there to go out on a date. Bet you I was not there when they returned. I called one of my home boys, rented a U-Haul and packed up all my shit. Everything I came in the house with. I had two weeks left in school and I was not going to spend them uncomfortable in that house. So, me and my things were gone. TV, living room furniture, utensils, and dining room table. We had been taking care of each other for so long, we always said what is yours, is mine. But that day I was done. Hauled ass to my cousin's house on the beach and was there until my departure. Once she returned home of course she was mad. Wanted to fight. She could not believe I would make such a move. As I reflected, I knew I could have handled it differently. But as a twenty-year-old who was hurt and felt alone this was the outcome.

Once I packed up and returned home for Christmas break, I informed my family of the school change. "Oh, by the way, when we return to school, I'll be going to Tallahassee and attending FAMU". They were shocked. Stunted even. Asking all kinds of questions and wanting to know what I needed them to do. The answer was nothing. It was handled. I had an apartment at university gardens and a schedule. My cousins already attended, and my big brother was re-enrolling. Gerry had been out of school for about a year and decided to return when I applied. Like I said, we had it all under control. The school had my ideal major, and I made a conscious decision to go and be greater.

On January 3, 2011 I touched down in Tallahassee, fl. Arrived at university gardens and signed my lease. Unpacked my clothes and headed over to Bernard. Bernard aka Berny is our adopted cousin from our days on the track. He lived three buildings down in the same complex. That semester I stayed at his house more than mine. Either way, I was now in town, so it was time to get my hoes in line. It was "real hot girl shit" before it was ever a thing. With one quick Facebook status update the messages started rolling in. "Dear Tallahassee, the Queen is here". A few friends from my childhood hit me up ASAP. "You here"? And just like that, we were back in the game. Those "hey big head" messages were on the way.

That semester I felt like a freshman all over again. New campus, new people, and a fresh atmosphere. As a health science major, I knew I was studying information that resonated with me. Even still, I managed to earn a "D" in anatomy. Majority of my time was spent in the gym getting in shape. My other time was spent on the sofa watching weeds with Bernard's roommate, Jaheem. Jaheem was my in-house husband. His last name was Jones so that was the running joke. He was a cool person and we bonded over tv. We would attend class and rush home to finish episodes. He made me watch weeds. I introduced him to the golden girls. That was honestly one of my favorite platonic relationships.

Being on the hill gave me a new start in life. Id switched schools, joined the rival team, and was now surrounded by family. I lived with my brother and cousin, had scheduled dates with Cousin Jas and attended the weekly parties on the set. It was spring at FAMU, so every day was a fashion show. Lines were coming out and the campus was overrun by DJs and club promoters. Attending shows hosted by the dance troops was the thing to do, and we found a reason to get lit every Friday night. We lived in UG so there was always a weekly fight. I witnessed cars being keyed, windows being smashed, liquor bottles being thrown, and a few people being dragged. Of all the college apartments I guess you could consider University Gardens the ghetto. But we loved every moment. It was drop season, so it was money in the city. All the girls carried big bags, boys rocked fitted caps and ray bans were the trend. It was a time in life one had to have been there to understand. It was the epitome of the HBCU experience and culture. Adding in that experience was Dr. Bell. the professor of educational psychology. She wore a dashiki to class every day and only rocked an afro. She began each lecture with a history lesson on Kemet and all things African. She ensured we knew the value in our brown skin and

Insisted that we treasured our melanin. Dr. Cook shared information that I found interesting, and Dr. Brown slept with his pupils. That spring semester was important to me because as eventful as it was, I was learning how to be a student. I frequented the library more often and began to take organized notes. I attended professor led study sessions and asked more questions. After five semesters in school, I was finally beginning to find my rhythm. I was putting in an effort to fight all thoughts and feelings of any form of imposter syndrome. I had vowed to take all the world's burdens off my shoulders. Could not be a perfectionist because I am not perfect. I'm not an expert because I don't know everything, and I had to drop the facade of superwoman because it wasn't my job to save the world. I am leaving that up to the Lord.

In the summer of 2011 Ms. Celine and Grammy drove up to Tallahassee to find us all a place. Gerry and I were together during the spring semester, but Aurora was across town at Tallahassee community college. The goal was to have us all under one roof. Which made sense. We were all raised together so we should be there to look out for each other. During their visit we secured a 3-bedroom 3-bathroom townhouse on McCaskill Rd. exactly one mile from campus. We all had our own space, Gerry, and Aurora both had vehicles and Aurora had food stamps. We were set. For a while at least. The utilities were in my name and I oversaw collecting from them and paying the bill each month. I was still unemployed and a full-time student, so I paid bills in advance each semester with my refund check. Whatever funds I had left over was my spending money. Ms. Celine and Grammy were sending money to Tallahassee to help Aurora pay her portion every month just like we weren't all their children. She had the food stamps and shopped for the house for a month or so. She then realized her stamps stretched further when she was only feeding herself. So, she began only shopping for herself. She went to shop on her own and housed all nonperishables in her room. Canned goods, juices, and seasonings. Cooked just enough for herself and refrigerated the rest. Makes sense when you are charged to look out for yourself. But not when the people you live with are supposed to be your siblings. As usual, Gerry and I looked out for each other. Neither of us were much of a cook, so we would scrape a few dollars together each night to find something to eat.

Outside of family I had not established too many friends on the hill, so I spent most of my time on the phone with Donovan and Chanelle. Staying abreast to how they were doing and what was new in their lives was important to me. I never wanted the distance to affect our friendships. They say friends are the family members we choose, and we had all chosen each other. Donovan was in the service and had recently purchased a motorcycle. Chanelle was back in school and progressing in her career at the sheriff's office. We were all doing well. I also had to keep up with the latest topics with daddy, nanny, Taylor, auntie and Christian. Not sure how I managed to keep up with it all with only 24 hours in a day. It was now the fall of 2011 and I added two more people to the roster. That semester, sitting in doctor holder's anatomy class in BL Perry I found my friends. I found Him. Houston Gilyard.

I walked in class late and in this auditorium style class, all the seats were taken. I walked all the way to the back, and he picked up his bag and said, "You can sit here". That was it. I was in. He looked up and flashed a slight smile, highlighted by a tiny gap. I was in love. He started a conversation by saying he thought we had more classes together. It made sense; we had the same major. If I'm being truthfully honest, I'd been smitten with him since the semester before. We both had Dr. Cooks class and I watched him walk in late every day. I thought he was cute then but the closer he would get my mind would always say, "damn Joness, that's a big bitch". And he was. Six foot, two inches, two hundred eighty pounds and solid. A Man. we talked and barely listened to the lecture as we got acquainted. He introduced me to a few of his acquaintances. One disadvantage of being a transfer student was not knowing the people you came in with. This class and those encounters made up for that. I began to accompany him and his friends in the rattlers den. We went straight there after class and he immediately became my spades partner. We shared our hopes and dreams and deepest admiration. They mirrored each other. We were both health science majors and wanted to work for professional sports teams. Over two months, he became my person. The one I looked for in class, spent time with talking trash and did not mind giving a helping hand. One evening while forming a study group he introduced me to Zion. A small framed red girl from Gainesville. We met up in the library the next evening preparing for an exam and she and I were the first two there. As we got situated, she looked up at me and said, "You drink. If so, you should come over". As simple as it was that was the start of a beautiful bond. She lived alone not too far from our home. I began to frequent her house often to study, gossip, drink and eat. She also had food stamps and loved to cook. She would even cook meals and drop them at the front door for Gerry and me on her way to work. She Instantly became family. We attended clubs some nights, hosted debate nights and vented about our relationship drama. If there was a scene to be on, we were there together, but we preferred to be ducked off.

On October 28, 2011 Donovan called me to give me an update about his motorcycle. I was not a fan of him riding because I thought it was dangerous. My opinion is not worth too much of anything because he was a grown man and could do as he pleased. That Sunday afternoon Chanelle called me and said, "what's wrong with Donovan "? My first thought was, "I told that boy not to get that damn bike. I was concerned but still nonchalant. I was not too worried because I figured it was not that bad. She told me to get on Facebook because people were writing, "R.I.P Donovan". I chuckled because I was not about to listen to Facebook. They kill people on Facebook every day. Not Donovan. I just knew he was alive. I called his phone nonstop with no reply. Called my parents and asked them to go to the local hospital to get me answers. They called me back one hour later with his mother on the phone who confirmed his time of death. Standing in our living room I immediately got weak. Aurora had to catch me before I hit the floor. I was numb. He was not the first person I have lost. In elementary school I lost Brielle who was struck by a car. At the age of eleven

I lost little granddaddy after a few bouts with strokes. In high school we lost granddaddy Walton after his struggle with high blood pressure, heart disease and diabetes. But Donovan, Donovan's death hit differently. He was the first man outside of my family to love me. We were friends. We were family. Just like Ms. Jordon predicted we were made for each other. I was just too stubborn and stuck in my ways. He'd been recently trying to express his feelings for me, and I would stop him every time. I loved and respected him too much to hurt him with my antics. As a college student I was enjoying the entertainment from other men. Was not ready to settle down yet. I had come to the realization that we may get there later in life. And in the blink of an eye the lord took that option away. I was weak, I was hurt, and in a house full of people, I felt alone. I stayed up crying the entire night. My family came in from around the city to check on my wellbeing. I was honestly in a very fragile state.

The next day at school Houston could tell there was something wrong with me and inquired about what was wrong immediately following class. I told him I lost my best friend. The story I received was he drove off on his motorcycle to show the bike to his friends and cousins. While he was gone, he lost control of the bike, hit a tree and experienced internal bleeding. I was angry and overcome with grief. Sunken in a mixture of feelings I was still happy it was Houston there consoling me. We walked through campus as he allowed me to vent. I'm sure it wasn't a level of ideal comfort for a 21-year-old young man to console a new friend crying over another man. But it was what I needed.

The following week was one of a rollercoaster of emotions. I felt disregarded, dismissed, jealous and like others diminished our relationship. I was not in the city so there was nothing I could do to help prepare for the weekend's events. His ex-girlfriend stepped in and filled the position I felt I should have been. At the funeral she sat up front and consoled his mother and even inherited his dog. In his obituary my name was mentioned next to last as if I was some sort of afterthought. We were never sexual, as a matter of fact we never shared a kiss. But we loved one another. Although he made it his business to begin something with all the females, I was close to. He defended himself saying if he couldn't have me, he figured my friends would be the closest version of the real thing. Now I was left on earth feeling like I had to defend our level of love. Following the funeral, I felt numb and stuck. Whenever I allowed others into my pain and grief, they encouraged me to get over it and move on as if they did not understand why I was hurt. So, I retreated into my room with nothing but the tv and food.

The following five semesters I experienced a functioning depression. I was numb and going through the motions. I attended class and stopped any forms of studying. After class all I did was sleep and eat. I was overeating, over drinking and constantly felt sick. The only emotions I felt were the ones I had for Houston. The time I spent with him I felt alive. The few hours I spent with him throughout the day were a glimpse of my former self. We talked for hours, laughed at ourselves and others and I felt safe. Every day he dropped me at my front door, and I felt my soul deflate. I was not secure on my own. In the moments alone I cried, asked God why and had suicidal thoughts. Only My love for my siblings and nephew kept me here. I was drowning and did not know how to ask for a raft.

The first person who noticed I was in distress was a professor. He asked me to stay after class one day and he said he felt that I was "off". I immediately began to shed tears that I could not stop. He collected my belongings and escorted me over to Sunshine Manor, the mental health facility on campus. We made a deal that I had to attend ten therapy sessions to continue in his class. I held up my end of the bargain. For the next ten Fridays I spent an hour on campus baring my soul. It was therapeutic and cleansing, but it wasn't a healing.

We continued clubbing for celebrations, over drinking and being promiscuous. I even had an encounter with a married man. Houston is who I wanted and who I invested myself with, but I ended each evening feeling unwanted, untouched, and less than. So, I filled the void with sporadic encounters with men I would never truly consider. It is not like men were not checking for me. I am jones. It is just that they aren't who I wanted. Since the day we met it was always him. He was the one I was feeling, and only his opinions mattered. But I was trying to combat my continued feeling of numbness with feeling something. Did not mean I slept with all these men. I honestly needed preoccupying my free time. Needed to distract my damaged heart and mind. In doing so I was also protected from feeling rejected whenever Houston was too busy. I am a woman, so you know how we do. Create scenarios and make assumptions. He was not touching me, so I knew it was someone. We were two and half years deep in a sexless situationship. We were friends, but everyone knew it was more than that. His friends became my family, he had grown close with mine and I was off the market. At least that is how it seemed. One of our male classmates told me because of Houston's stature and constant presence, other men were scared to approach me. That was cool. I was single but spoken for. As much as I wanted a title and relationship, I did not need it. I had lost all grips of me, how in the hell was I supposed to focus on us. Yet and still, I did. To be honest that is one of the reasons I'm still here. Without being a girlfriend or hopes of being a future Mrs. I registered for class, completed homework, brought groceries, and helped pay bills. Just another example of my emotional immaturity and repercussion of such a problematic past. Id grown so used to accepting whatever was given and not fighting for what I deserved or my respect. Throughout my life I have grown too content with the bare minimum. Either way, it Gave me a sense of purpose, a reason to keep moving forward. It was my seatbelt to keep me anchored here. I have been laughed at and ridiculed because of my decisions regarding our situation. According to others, I do too much, go out of my way and they do not see it reciprocated. I had to come to the realization that not everything is for everyone to witness or understand. He is caring and kind, hardworking, smart, and mostly honest. He is handsome, Hella sexy and understands me. In the pits of my depression and forty pounds larger, I still felt special.

My twenty third birthday was the essence of that. I made up in my mind that we were all going to go out to the moon to have a good time. Whenever we, Aurora, Zion, and I went out we rotated our drinks. Aurora's choice was gin. Zion's was patron. I drink Hennessey. That night, I wanted everyone to feel exactly how they wanted. So, I went to the liquor store and purchased them all. We spent the afternoon looking for an outfit in governor square mall. I grabbed a shirt for Houston since he was at work. Dropped it off at his place since he would miss pregame. That evening, we were lit, and it was up there. We started off with Zion's pina coladas laced with patron. We ate the food Aurora made and slowly got ready as we were taking sips. After two cups Aurora said, "nah, you not where I want you to be. Fix her another one z". So, I began to down my third cup. I was taking shots of Hennessey with everyone in the house in the moment in between. Once we were fully dressed and preparing to depart, we had all reached our limits. But I was a little further into my intoxication than others. Before I stepped foot out of the front door, I consumed three pina coladas and six shots. A recipe for disaster. We arrived at the moon after a car ride full of jokes and laughs. I walked through the front door and approached Houston who beat us there. With a laugh I pulled him close and said, "We've been pregaming for hours, you need to catch up". He invited me over to the bar and proceeded to order drinks. "Aye, let me get six double shots of Hen". I remember standing there rationing the drinks out in my head. "Okay. Me, Houston, Gerry, Aurora, Z and Bernard. Six, Cool". Before I finished my thought, he downed three and pushed the rest to me. "Now you catch up". It was not like me to back down from a challenge. So, without hesitation and no regard for the rest of the night, I downed each one and walked back towards the dance floor. I was gone. I remember dancing to one song after that. The rest of the night is a blur. According to everyone, that is because I blacked out and fell on the dancefloor. Together, they carried me up three flights of stairs to ensure I got my picture. That captured moment is priceless and timeless and depicts how I was obviously not standing on my own. My entourage all squeezed towards the middle to help support me. On the way down the steps, as Houston attempted to pick me up, the effort also lifted my tight dress. Naturally, Bystanders were preceding to record me. I was the drunk bitch in the bar. It was horrible and humiliating, but I had a team who loved me. Houston threw me into my brother and cousin who honestly could not handle my dead weight. He did so in one swift move swing at a dude. He said he told buddy to put down his phone and those were the consequences since he did not listen. Although we were already leaving, we ended up getting escorted out. Once we made it back to our house, they all got me on the toilet so I could relieve myself. With all those drinks in me, I had not once peed. They got me back into the living room and proceeded to have a photoshoot. Aurora, Zion, Houston, and Gerry were enjoying a drunken laugh. I was passed out on the floor as they took pictures with me. Houston sat me on the sofa, and I hit my head on the armrest and busted my lip. There was blood everywhere. Once I rose from my drunken slumber the next morning I was confused and in pain. I had no recollection of what happened. As I heard my brother in the front room moving around, I called out to him. "Brother, did I show my ass like I think I did"? He walked into his room and chuckled, "Yeah you did. Literally". The sad part was my actual birthday was not until Monday. I walked into class with a swollen lip and bruised. Their fingerprints were all over my body from them attempting to hold me. No one in my class believed that I did not get my ass beat. Even after that poor display of composure and womanhood, between Houston and I, nothing changed. I was over myself and embarrassed. He was there to witness that I could not handle myself. Still, he continued to treat me with care, gave me love daily and made sure others respected me.

Not too long after my birthday, Aurora helped save my life. We have never been truly close and failed to exist as sisters. But I will always give credit where it is due. One random day, she busted in my room and insisted on making me move. She drug me out of bed and suggested we go into the neighborhood and take a walk. She did the same thing for a few weeks. She was overly annoying and opened my dark curtains. "Alright sis, it's time to get out of this house". She would say, "I don't care what we go do, but we have to do something". When all I wanted to do is lay there and continue to exist, she made me live again. With her help, I slowly walked out of my almost three-year depression. I gradually rejoined society and our relationship was improving. Taylor and I have always been close, but that is because she was my baby. In our circumstance, I was forced to be her mother. So, we shared a different love. Were more than sisters. Were mother and daughter. Were best friends. Aurora and I would be good for moments and spend longer time on the outs. She would get random attitudes and not speak to me. Never understood why. But right then, she thought enough of me to save me. And for that, I will always be appreciative.

Before long I was in Tallahassee somewhat alone. Gerry returned to Miami, Zion returned to Gainesville and Aurora stopped speaking to me when she moved out.
Without a third person, we could no longer afford rent, so our lease was over. I began working at Avis and moved in with our cousin Lawrence. I had one more semester in school and he opened his door. He allowed me to live with him rent free as I refocused and continued my journey. I was close to graduation and during my rebirth began to fear the real world. I had been a student my entire life. I feared graduating and walking into the real world unemployed and ill prepared. I called my mother's baby brother. Uncle burger had made a career out of the military. I was not military material but was willing to conform if it meant guaranteed consistency. I would have a place to stay and a guaranteed check. Would not have to fight for underpaid positions and would have my own health insurance. I was sold. Applying for the coast guard and officer candidate school was now the goal. After speaking with a Jacksonville recruiter, I was given the runaround for about a month. He jotted down my height and weight and was

done entertaining me. At that time, I was twenty-four years old, 5'5" and two hundred and sixty-five pounds. The largest id ever been. I just needed to know the requirements so I could set my goals. To be eligible for OCS I would have to be at a max of 165, run two miles nonstop, along with two-minute pushups and sit ups. I began by walking a few miles a day at the lake. I slowly incorporated a 45-minute full body workout video. Four days a week I did two- a -days and went to the campus gym. I was on a mission. I was getting in shape and rehabbing my GPA. I damn near lived in the library during the time I was not in the gym or at work. For the first time in life, my own success was finally the priority. It was not Deon's grades, my family's needs, or daddy's health. I was learning how to take care of myself. Still, it took some intervention from my uncle to get the recruiters attention. After a brief conversation of me explaining my dilemma he said, "Just sit by the phone". Two minutes later my phone rang, and the recruiter was on the other end, "Ms. Pratt we had no clue you were the niece of Commander Jordan". From that point on they rolled out the red carpet. They ensured I was working in the right direction and began preparing my formal packet. At that point I was three courses away from graduation, running two and a half miles a day and eighty pounds lighter. I cut off all my hair and never felt better. I was more involved in church and following all the great advice I received from my baby brother. When I looked in the mirror, I finally saw the woman the little girl in me always wanted to be.

I was employed, in shape, getting grades, growing closer to the Lord and confident. I was living in a bubble that was drama free. I also stopped conversing with other men. If they were not feeding my soul or promoting my growth, I didn't want any parts of it. I was gossiping less and praying more. And doing it all while pulling Houston along. I ensured we took the necessary classes and submitted our applications for graduation on time. Having him with me was an additional form of self-care. He was my right hand, partner and go to. Ensuring we both crossed the stage was not up for debate.

December approached fast and it felt like a whirlwind. Auntie Ari created my graduation invitations and corralled major support from my dysfunctional family. Everyone prepared to meet and support me on the highest of seven hills. Christian flew in first. We had all witnessed him graduating from college in 2013. Taylor was in college at Jackson state and would arrive later with the family. Auntie, uncle Lawrence and Grandma Walton drove in from Albany. Gerry drove up from south Florida and even picked up cookie in Tampa on his way. My mother was in the car with auntie Arianna, and Cousin Celest. I had not heard from Aurora in months, and she even gave me a call so she could be involved. Chanelle and Terrell came up the road to ensure I felt their love. On December 12, 2014 I woke up with a sense of achievement. In all that I had endured I was still standing. I was wiser, I was stronger. I was whole. Before my hectic preparations I took a praise break. I found myself exclaiming songs including, "He's Able", ``More than a conquer, and "Blessing in the Storm". Regardless of how my story started, all my bad decisions or pain I've tried to ignore, the Lord kept me. He protected me from others. More importantly, he guarded me from myself. In twenty-four years, I'd experienced mental, physical, and emotional abuse. Survived loss, depression, and grief. I was no longer the "fat friend" and was loved by a man. I was happy and the best part about it was, I was still growing. As I prepared for graduation, I knew the day's celebrations were greater than myself. That day was for my village. For the ones who drug me through the mud and placed me on a pedestal. I completed what my mother could not. As much as I hate to admit it, I probably would not have finished without her.

I encompass all her best attributes and a determination only formed because circumstances snowballed by her. I knew I deserved better because of the lifestyle we once lived and because my siblings insisted, I was a Queen. This degree was for them. For my daddy, grandparents, and aunts. For my god mothers and friends. For the ones I had lost and for the ones still there holding my hand. I was not head of my class or summa cum laude. But I was there. I finished school with a 2.95 cumulative G.P.A. again, Almost great, but still not quite good enough. Yet and still, I earned a 3.3 in the last sixty credits of my degree.

On December 12th I walked into the Al Lawson multipurpose gymnasium as a candidate for graduation for the commencement of Fall of 2014. I was followed closely by the man the Lord knew I would one day need. At 6:00pm the ceremony began and by 8:00pm I had a conferred degree in health science from the greatest HBCU in the nation. That entire weekend we partied, gave thanks, cried, and ate. The weekend came to an end and this was my final statement, *"As I prepare for church this morning, I am reflecting on my graduation weekend and I can honestly say that I am blessed beyond measure. Over the past four days I have laughed, cried, partied hard and prayed even harder. Enjoyed the company of an abundance of family and friends and received kind gifts and kinder words. I have completed one chapter and am preparing for the next. I entered Bethune Cookman University as a child and I graduated from the greatest HBCU in the nation, a blessed woman. I represent Florida Agricultural & Mechanical University October 3, 1887 WHAT!?".*

At the age of twenty-four and a college graduate I submitted the following letter of intent to the United States Coast Guard OCS:

I have learned throughout life's numerous lessons that there are not any perfect circumstances, only ordinary people who have been properly prepared to conform amidst technical hitches. Every decision made, action taken, and all habits formed are liable to affect surrounding relationships and future endeavors. As a recent college graduate, I have approached an era which will ultimately define all forthcoming details of my lifetime. I would consider it an esteemed privilege to be extended the opportunity to become a candidate for officer in the United States Coast Guard. With the assistance of a profound educa-

tional background, proven dedication to enhancement of the community and established resilience when confronted with incomparable circumstances I believe I have been groomed for servant leadership and would be honored to be of service to my country.

"A good education is the greatest gift you can give yourself or anyone else". As a product of the inner city of Tampa, FL I was continually urged to yearn for educational opportunities in efforts to advance intellectually as well as socially. The only method to improve mentally, physically, and spiritually; individually and as a community is to grasp a deeper understanding of the essential areas of academia while attempting to achieve a level of self-actualization. As a student at George S. Middleton High School, I recognized my potential for advancement in the health science program while continuing work towards my high school diploma. While in the program I assumed a leadership role on the Health Occupation Students of America executive board as well as a group spearhead throughout clinical training. Following graduation, I received a high school diploma as well as became a certified first responder. Primary general education credits were earned at the prestigious Bethune Cookman University as a biology student. After four collegiate semesters and personal maturity I transferred to Florida A&M University where I received my Bachelor of Science degree in Health Science Pre-Occupational Therapy. Throughout my collegiate career I have gained an immense amount of knowledge and look forward to continuing in this fashion as a member of the United States Coast Guard.

"The high destiny of the individual is to serve rather than to rule". Since my departure from high school, I pledged to lead my life in a way reflecting one of servant leadership as designated by author Robert Greenleaf. Community enhancement is the simplest manner to promote societal advancement and progress. As a freshman in Daytona Beach, FL I volunteered at the Chiles Academy assisting pregnant teens and teen mothers in their attempt to gain their high school diploma. Dedicating three days a week to four young ladies I served as an academic tutor and life mentor. The following academic year I served as a peer mentor for incoming freshmen at Bethune Cookman University who required assistance in reading and writing via the Wildcats Write initiative. This project enabled me to support individuals who were transitioning into university life and unaware of the abundant number of resources available to them. After transferring to Florida A&M University in Tallahassee, FL I participated in projects serving food at "The Shelter" on Saturday mornings with classmates, aided in building homes for Habitat for Humanity with Jacob Chapel Missionary Baptist Church young adult ministry and contributed to countless volunteer agendas with the Health Science Pre-Physical Therapy Association. I believe I have been called to serve in all capacities of life and have confidence it is now my duty to serve my country.

"Man never made a material as resilient as the human spirit". We all have our own individual battles we must encounter daily. With each obstacle designed to destroy our confidence and spirit we must acquire the lessons and continue to persevere. Throughout my lifespan I have survived familial drama, financial difficulties, struggles in certain

academic areas and the loss of a lifelong friend. These happenstances all impacted me enough to force me to remain humble but never enough to break my spirit. I now know that we must endure trials and tribulations caused by friends and family, have a sense of money consciousness until we gain financial freedom, place an added effort in any area of life in which we do not possess a particular talent and a life lost is a lesson learned. After the loss of my friend, I grieved for an extended period and just recently accepted reality. Taking back control of my life I have lost eight five pounds through hard work and dedication, refocused my goals and completed my undergraduate degree. Now I am prepared to move forward academically, in innovative leadership capacities and to face different responsibilities and challenges.

My future was now in a state of limbo, but I was not afraid. It was up to me to work hard and pray. The Lord would work the rest out in my favor. Just as he had done so before.

To my children who have served as a motivation to complete this project, I offer you a few words of wisdom. Listen to the old folks. They have gone, did and survived similar experiences. Their sole purpose is not to spoil your fun, rather to save you from some heart aches and pain. When you encounter dark times, know that you are not alone. Anchor yourselves in a higher power. I, recommend Jesus. Keep at least one good friend, foster healthy relationships and love people while you can. When in need, seek some form of therapy and learn to vocalize your feelings. A title Ain't everything but still know your worth. Treat people with respect and know that the world owes you nothing. You cannot be afraid to work, and you'll benefit from developing resilience. Be kind and respect authority. Family is family, either built or by blood. Find your niche and foster it. Value education, life will only be what you make it. Forgive your parents, they are only human and trying to get through life too. Finally, if your dreams don't give you that bubble gut feeling, go back to the drawing board. Dream bigger.

I am not famous or rich. I just know everyone has a story, and up until now, this has been mine. Some Things Are Greater Than Ourselves. Some Truths Are Lived to Be Told. Silence Is Self-Betrayal That Impedes on Generational Growth. Some people will hate me for telling it. Others have constantly reminded me that mine has not been the worst. I am not here to point fingers, place blame or garner pity. For me, this has been therapy. I needed to get it out of my mind and off my chest. Whoever it blesses in the process is an additional advantage. I need people to know that we are not our circumstances. We are not here to live in the shadows of our parents' problems. You will not crucify me for the sins of my mother and father. They must carry their own burdens and vices. As you have read through my young adult years, I have enough mess of my own to take to my Lord. This was not their story. I am not responsible for that. This was how I experienced them. How I experienced it all. How I survived childhood trauma and managed to still be here. How I had to reconcile with the dumb decisions I made as a young adult and use those same experiences to sew into children daily. If we wallow in who we are in our lowest moments, we will never recognize our greatest potential. At 30, I have loved, been loved, had my hoe moments, and been played. I have been the judgmental friend and the dumb bitch stuck on the same man. I have hurt men. Hell, I've hurt myself. I have been a disrespectful child and an even worse granddaughter at times. I have made awful financial decisions and bounced back with a credit score better than a lot of the rest. Some pain I've internalized and will take to my grave. Majority, I have decided to share with the world. However, one of the greatest lessons I have learned is taking accountability for my own shit. Some things are inevitable, other things we bring on ourselves. Ultimately, I intend on making it through both, just the same. Ten toes down and above the ground. If you only take one thing away from this lifetime of mine, take this. Remain humble enough to be human and on any given day, yall do me a favor, Go Be Great.

Now how is that for a little Summer Fun?

P.S. #MeToo. Nevertheless, She Persisted. -

Become A Freebie By Joining The Conversation In Our Virtual Book Club At Https:// Www.summerfunbook.com/

1. Quick history lesson for the children.
The crack era- what was it, when was it and how did it affect us as a community?

2. Have you ever wondered what happened to the children of the crack era? We know some of the addicts went to rehab, some succumbed to overdose and others are still battling the addiction today. But what happened to their offspring?

3. "What happens in this house, stays in this house". Does it hurt us, or does it help us? Where did it come from and who does it benefit?

4. We've all experienced things that made such an impact on our lives that it helped shape who we are today. Those detrimental things that determine how we see the world and experience people. Which would you say affected you more, the things you've done and decisions you made or dramatic events within your nuclear family?

5. What Is Mental Health to you?

6. Genetic Predisposition for Substance Abuse (Bad Blood) and generational curses. Are they real? Do we believe in them? How do we break them?

Back Cover

Born and raised in the inner city of Tampa, Fl
Joness is no stranger to drama or trauma. Born into a life
of sadistic unfortunate events she had to battle her parents' addictions, inevitable anxiety, and a lifelong feeling
of imposter syndrome. Nevertheless, she persisted. As a
graduate of FAMU and FIU respectively, she now gives her
time, talent, and efforts where it's needed the most. As an
athletic trainer in the inner city, she makes a conscious decision to be the adult she once needed. This is for the love
of the children and every adult recovering from traumatic
events. You survived the abuse, surely you can survive the
recovery

Joness: I'm Not Famous or Rich...

Student: Well, You Famous on Campus. We Be Calling Your Name All Day. And You Rich in Love. I Think You Winning

Moral: PERSPECTIVES